DESPERADO

WONDER HORSE BOOK THREE

BY

VICTORIA HARDESTY
AND
NANCY PEREZ

PO Box 221974 Anchorage, Alaska 99522-1974
books@publicationconsultants.com—www.publicationconsultants.com

ISBN Number: 978-1-59433-818-2
eBook ISBN Number: 978-1-59433-819-9

Copyright 2018 Victoria Hardesty and Nancy Perez
—First Edition—

Manufactured in the United States of America

This book is dedicated to all those young men
who ever loved a horse and
spent every waking minute they had with their
own Wonder Horse.

OTHER BOOKS

by Victoria Hardesty and Nancy Perez

PRINCE ALI – Wonder Horse Book One

LA DUQUESA – Wonder Horse Book Two

ACKNOWLEDGEMENTS

We could never complete a manuscript without our Beta Readers. We want to thank Rebecca Gordon and Sharon Zaragoza for their invaluable assistance in refining our work, helping get us out of our "comma coma" and their insightful suggestions for content.

We also need to thank members of the National Forest Service in Colorado for their help with the flora in the region where this story takes place. We thank Professor Google for help in setting up a strong north wind based on weather patterns and cold and warm fronts and the way they behave. Professor Google also helped us with the animals likely to be found in the area and gave us a lot of information about scuba diving!

We appreciate friends and family members who supported us in our efforts to write a series of books and especially our husbands, Mike and Ray, for giving us the time we needed to actually accomplish what we have so far.

CHAPTER ONE

Desperado had some time to think. It was before dawn Sunday morning after the Finals on Saturday night in Albuquerque, New Mexico. He'd been there for over a week for the Arabian Youth National Championship Show with his rider, Todd O'Neal. Of course, Todd was his best friend in all the world not just his rider. They'd competed in four classes that week and took the Championship trophy for three of them and a Third Place in the fourth class. Desperado didn't mind at all they'd placed behind Prince Ali with Becky and La Duquesa with Maryann in the Showmanship class. He'd known Prince Ali since he arrived at Cold Water Creek Ranch for training. He knew Becky well. He'd never met La Duquesa before but liked her very much. She was a classy mare in all respects. He liked her friend Maryann also.

Desperado's mind wandered a bit. He remembered the long meandering trail rides he'd taken with Todd in the foothills of the Rocky Mountains. He'd gone on rides with Prince Ali and Becky many times. They usually ended up at their "magic meadow". A clear freshwater creek ran alongside the meadow and eventually joined Boulder Creek a few miles downstream of the ranch. He considered Prince Ali a buddy and he enjoyed Becky too.

That brought him to another thought. Prince Ali was lucky. He belonged to his best friend. He knew Becky and Prince Ali would never be separated. That wasn't his situation at all. He belonged to Hilda Jorgensen who was in her 80's and frail health. He'd been taken to Cold Water Creek Ranch soon after Hilda's husband, Jan, passed away. Desperado missed Jan terribly. He remembered all the times he'd given Jan fits. He could escape his stall no matter what type of latch Jan put on it. He pulled Jan's cap off his head and tossed it across the barn in fun. He played tricks on him every chance he got and even did some with Hilda when he could get by with it. Those were the days. He'd been quite young. He loved the Jorgensens, but his heart now and forever belonged to Todd O'Neal.

The problem was Hilda was getting old. Her two adult children had come to the barn on a couple of occasions to see him while he was in training. Her children only came to please their mother. They had absolutely no interest in him. He'd overhead several short conversations, out of Hilda's hearing of course, where they'd said so. He knew if Hilda passed away, her children would sell him off as quickly as they could and for as much money as possible. He had no control over that. He knew it would break his heart.

Desperado tried to concentrate on the here and now. Whenever Todd rode him in competition Desperado put his best hoof forward. He never bobbled. His spins were straight and true with perfect stops. His flying lead changes were perfection. His Western Pleasure headset was flawless. He never bobbed his head or swished his tail no matter what. He always picked up the correct lead no matter which direction they traveled in. His gait changes were smooth and barely perceptible. He concentrated hard for Todd. He never messed up a class. Every time they competed as a team they won. He didn't realize that complicated matters more and more. Every time they won, his monetary value increased. It placed him farther and farther away from anything Todd could afford. Now, at the Nationals Show, he'd won three national titles. If things were difficult for Todd before it was nearly impossible now. He didn't understand it. He did his very best for Todd because he wanted to belong to him and he wanted to please Todd.

Fourteen-year-old Todd O'Neal had the best experience of his life at the Youth Nationals. He'd won the Championship trophies for Reining, Western Pleasure and Western Dressage for riders fourteen and over. He also brought home a Top Ten Ribbon for Showmanship, all with his best friend Desperado. Every time he thought about it he went into Desperado's stall and hugged him again and gave him a treat.

The Youth Championship show ended Saturday night. Today was take-down day. Everything had to be packed up and stowed in trucks, trailers, and cars before the horses loaded. Cold Water Creek Ranch from Boulder, Colorado and Hartley Ranch from Pinon Hills, California went together in one barn at the New Mexico State Fairgrounds. Chris and Sharon O'Neal from Colorado and Ginny Hartley from California were close friends and put their barns together because they shared an interest in Prince Ali. Chris had been his trainer from the time he was a yearling. Ginny Hartley was the riding coach for Becky Howard, Ali's best friend.

Everyone checked out of the hotel early Sunday morning so they could pack and leave for home. The food vendors at the fairgrounds were still putting out dishes from every culture that morning to feed hungry participants packing up their gear. The group from both ranches had breakfast at the fairgrounds while they worked.

The young competitors were bouncy and energetic that morning. The Championship Show had gone well for them all. Every single one had brought home a Championship, Reserve Championship, Third Place Trophy or Top Ten ribbons meaning they were among the top riders in North America in their discipline for their age group. The ribbons and trophies were carefully wrapped and protected from damage. They were the most important things to bring home next to their horses.

Todd and Becky were in the ready room next to Desperado's stall chattering away as they packed. "You know I'm the only kid competing in our group that doesn't own his horse," Todd told Becky. "You are so lucky. No one will ever sell Prince Ali to someone else."

"Gosh, I hadn't thought of that," Becky said. "You're right though. Now that Maryann's grandparents gave her La Duquesa, you are the only one of us riding a horse that belongs to someone else. Can't your dad and mom buy Desperado for you?"

"Probably not now," Todd answered. "I've thought about offering Hilda Jorgenson my allowance and getting a part-time job so I could buy him myself. That's if she'd let me make payments. Problem is every time he wins, his value goes up. Now there's no way I can ever afford him with three National Championships." Todd hesitated and stared out the doorway with a sad look on his face.

"Oh, no! Todd, there must be something you can do," Becky suggested. "You two belong together. Everyone who sees you riding can tell that."

"This isn't getting the packing done. Guess we'd better get back at it," Todd sighed and resumed the work.

Desperado heard every word of that conversation. He didn't know what to think. When he rode with Todd he didn't want to let him down, so he put his best into every ride. Apparently, that was the wrong thing to do because it sounded like it would be impossible for him to ever belong to Todd now. It made him sad. He decided he'd talk to Prince Ali when they got to the ranch. He was smart. Maybe he'd have an idea.

While everyone rushed through packing, Todd had a great idea. It cheered him up. He mentioned it to Becky and Maryann Wilcox who happened to be in the ready room with him at the same time.

"Wouldn't it be fun if you guys all came to Colorado for a couple of days so we could trail ride next to the Rocky Mountains?" he suggested with a smile.

Becky jumped on the idea. She had been to Cold Water Creek Ranch many times over the past four years. "Yeah, if we could talk our parents into a trip to Colorado for a couple days, you and I could lead the rest out to that little brook beside the "magic meadow" and have lunch out there," she said. "That would be so much fun! Maybe some of the California girls can see a wolverine or a bobcat or an elk."

"I've never been to Colorado," Maryann said. "I'd love to see the Rocky Mountains. Riding Quesa there would be so much fun."

Word spread from one to another until all nine of the kids, including Brody Hartley, were sold on the idea. They started to work on their parents about it. Some of the parents were a hard sell because they had other obligations at home to get back to. Some, like Maryann's mother Rose, didn't and were easy to convince. Even Maryann's grandparents were push-overs about the idea. By 10:30 that morning, the group was split about fifty-fifty. Chris and Ginny talked about it privately.

"These kids put in a heck of a lot of hard work just to get to this show," Chris said. "I would love to have them at the ranch for a day or two. This might be a good reward for all their work."

"We can't all stay at your ranch. Some of these people have younger kids along with them too. Where would we all stay for a couple of nights?" Ginny asked.

"There are several lodges on the highway close to the ranch. During the winter they are always booked up. This is July and there's not a speck of snow worth skiing on the slopes near my place. The lodges are all vacant. I could call Sharon and ask her to check. Maybe she can wrangle a good deal from the owners. Right now they aren't making anything on empty properties," Chris suggested. "Some of the owners are friends of ours. They'll give us a good deal."

"That sounds like a great idea. Give Sharon a call and see what she can find. We can talk to the adults over lunch. If there's enough interest, we can do a detour on the way home."

"Yeah, and I'll let them know my place is only a seven-hour drive. We can be there early tonight. I have room for all the horses. Let's see what Sharon comes up with. I'll let you know," Chris told Ginny while he hauled another packed trunk out of the ready room.

In fact, Sharon was able to find three nice lodges that were vacant. The owners would love to fill them for a couple of days on short notice. They were also willing to drop their rates for this group. Sharon told them she would call them back within the hour to confirm and called Chris with the information.

Chris and Ginny got the adults together to discuss making a detour to Colorado. When they heard how little it was going to cost, they agreed. It would be a nice reward for the kids who'd worked so hard. It would only delay them two more days and give them some vacation time. The packing finished before lunch. The kids wandered the fairgrounds for an hour to say goodbye to new friends they'd made from different parts of the country. Then they hurried back to load the horses.

The caravan got underway just after 1:00 that afternoon with Chris leading and Charlie Reeves parents in the rear position so they could help any stragglers that missed a turn. Charlie and his parents lived a short distance from Chris's ranch. The procession drove through the front gates of Cold Water Creek Ranch a little after 8:00 that evening in time to watch the sunset as the horses were bedded down for the night. Sharon rode in the lead car to the lodges and helped get everyone checked in, two families per lodge. Sharon knew the owners, being neighbors and friends for years.

The lodges were fully furnished private homes with multiple bedrooms, fold-out couches, bunk beds, large living rooms and kitchens complete with linens and dishware. That afternoon, Sharon put in a few supplies so they had cereal, toast, milk, and coffee for the morning. She promised to take the moms shopping the next day for groceries while the kids went for their ride.

Caroline and Walter Howard stayed with the O'Neal's. They were like family and stayed with them many times over the years while Prince Ali was in training with Chris. Becky had her own room at the ranch because she stayed there over Christmas, spring breaks and summer vacations. She didn't like being separated from her best friends, Prince Ali and Todd O'Neal.

Before leaving for the night, breakfast was scheduled for the morning. Moms and Grandma planned to help Sharon cook for the group and handle the clean-up. The Dads and Grandpa would get a tour of the ranch and help the kids get ready for their ride. Sharon and Caroline Howard stayed up a bit later packing sandwiches, cookies and crackers, small bags of chips and sodas the kids could take for their lunch in the woods.

Sharon and Caroline had been friends since college. While they worked, they caught up on events since Becky got out of the hospital. In March that year, Prince Ali was the Grand Marshall of the Swallows Day Parade in the Howard's hometown of San Juan Capistrano, California. After the parade two criminals put Becky in a coma with a concussion and stole Prince Ali. Sharon flew to California and stayed at the Howard's home so Walter and Caroline could stay with Becky at the hospital. In the meantime, it seemed the whole world looked for the 2.5-million-dollar stallion, Prince Ali. He showed up on his own at Ginny Hartley's ranch over a hundred miles from where he'd been stolen! It was such an astounding coincidence. Ginny was in San Juan Capistrano with Sharon helping care for the Howards herd of Arabian horses. Ginny coached Becky and Ali for the Youth Nationals before and again after the tragedy. The showing Becky and Ali did at Youth Nationals set everything right in their world again. The women prayed nothing like that would ever happen again.

CHAPTER TWO

Regardless of how late everyone got to bed the first night in Colorado, the kids were awake and up at the crack of dawn. The ones not at the ranch took advantage of the cereal and milk Sharon left the day before while they waited on their parents and siblings to get dressed. All they wanted to do was get to the ranch and ride!

Cars and trucks turned through the gates of Cold Water Creek Ranch before 7:00 a.m. that morning. The women hurried to the kitchen to prepare a large breakfast for the group while the kids visited the barn, checked on their horses and looked at horses in training. Todd and Becky gave the kids the grand tour of the facilities while Chris's morning crew fed the horses and cleaned stalls. They told their friends about their experiences riding off the ranch and told them about running into bears, badgers and wolverines, coyotes and bobcats, elk, and mule and whitetail deer. They might have embellished a bit. Charlie and Becky had ridden with Todd many times before. The girls from California could hardly wait. Their trail rides were in the desert where all they saw were rabbits, ground squirrels, and an occasional coyote. None of them had ever seen a live bear, wolverine, bobcat or elk.

The ladies flipped French toast on the grill, browned potatoes and fried bacon and sausages. They buttered toast, brewed coffee and heated up hot chocolate. All the while, those from California watched the elk and deer feeding in the meadow behind the ranch. It was something they never saw at home. The men of the group sat on the rear deck enjoying the view while they argued sports and politics. The younger siblings were all in Todd's playroom playing his video games.

When breakfast was ready, Sharon went out the mudroom door and rang the dinner bell. People trooped in and helped themselves. The group filled up the O'Neal's large dining and living rooms with lively conversation as they ate. The young competitors ate their breakfasts in a hurry. They couldn't wait to get started.

The barn was a madhouse with nine young riders tacking up their horses for the ride. Chris let Brody ride Sharon's personal horse so he could join the others. Brody didn't compete in New Mexico but joined Ginny to help the others wherever he could. He didn't want to miss the ride either. Sharon and Caroline handed each one a bag lunch which they stowed in pouches tied behind their saddles. Chris came into the barn to speak with Todd and Becky before the group left.

"You told me you are going to the brook southwest of the ranch and you plan to have lunch in the meadow there, right?" he asked Todd.

"Yeah, dad. I know the kids from California will like that place. Becky and Charlie agree with me," Todd answered.

"With this large a group, it's important that you all stay together. Don't let anyone wander off somewhere and get lost. We don't need to call Search and Rescue out to find you. How about we plan for you to be back here by 1:30 this afternoon? That should give you plenty of time for a good ride and a nice lunch by the brook, okay?" Chris asked. "Just remember some of the kids are not used to the wildlife out here or the terrain."

"We promise," Becky said. "Todd and Charlie and I will keep an eye on the others, so nobody gets lost."

"Okay, Becky, one more thing. Don't change your plans about where you are going. If I need to find you, I need to know where to look," Chris cautioned them.

"Okay, Dad," Todd and Becky said simultaneously and grinned at him. "We're just going to the brook southwest and the meadow. You know the one; it's the one we always go to. We won't go anywhere else. We'll see you at 1:30 or before."

With that, Todd led the way out of the barn and across the ranch to the rear gate. Charlie took up a position at the rear and Becky stayed in the middle of the pack. Todd leaned over and opened the rear gate from Desperado's back. He led the riders through. Charlie closed the gate after them. They walked through the meadow single file. Todd found the trail and started down it. The group stopped frequently to take pictures on their cell phones. It took them a while to reach the meadow beside the brook. Charlie and Todd set up a tie line between trees so they could tie their horses to it and leave them enough slack to graze on the fresh grass in the meadow. Some of the kids took their boots off and waded into the brook. It was cold and clear and felt good. The brown trout in the brook went into hiding.

The wildlife in the area avoided the meadow. The young people were enjoying themselves so there was a lot of laughing, joking and splashing going on. They created a racket that cleared the forest for a quarter of a mile. It was a beautiful day with the temperature in the seventy-five-degree range with lots of sunshine and blue sky. Puffy white clouds formed above the mountain peaks west of the ranch. Even though the forest around their private meadow still suffered from the drought of the past several years, the Pine trees were fragrant enough to remind the young people of the Christmas season. The stands of Aspen and Alder trees near the brook were in full leaf. They seemed to shudder in the breeze. Even the horses were in high spirits with the sunshine and fresh grass to munch on.

"Where are we going next," Suzie asked when things quieted down in the meadow. The kids had finished their lunch except for stray packages of crackers and bags of chips. They were a little sleepy from the meal, the sunshine, the exertion and the let-down from the prior week. They lay on their backs in the grass staring at the clouds above the mountains. After a while, several of the girls were ready to mount up and ride some more before they had to get back to the ranch for the day.

"Hey, you heard my dad," Todd reminded them. "We're not supposed to go off exploring. If our parents need us, they need to know where to look for us."

Becky said, "This is a pretty wild place. We don't want to stray too far just in case. Chris told us to go here and not go anywhere else."

"Aww, come on! We don't have to go far. I just want to see a badger, wolverine or a bobcat before we leave," Suzie whined. "I've never seen one of them or the mule deer or elk."

Several of the other kids shared Suzie's opinion. They argued about it for a while. Todd and Becky stood firm. Charlie, Maryann, and Brody joined them. Suzie finally snapped at Todd. "What? Are you afraid of your daddy, little boy?"

Heidi sneered at the naysayers. "Who's going to know anyway? We'll never tell."

"It doesn't matter!' Becky said. "Chris told us to stay together and not go anywhere other than what we discussed in case one of our parents needs to reach us before we get back to the ranch."

Suzie took Heidi's comments to mean she agreed with her. "Come on Heidi. Let's leave the babies here. We'll go sightseeing on our own." She turned her horse around and put her heels in his side. The horse jumped forward and began to canter up the trail. Heidi put her heels in her own horse and joined her.

"Now what are we going to do?" Todd asked as he watched the two girls getting smaller and smaller the farther up the trail they went.

Charlie watched the girls for a minute and said, "Todd we can't leave them on their own. What if a bull elk steps onto the path in front of them, or a mountain lion or something like that. They have no idea what to do or where to go. We're going to have to chase them down and bring them back to the ranch."

Becky agreed with Charlie. "Todd, he's right. We can't leave them on their own."

Brody spoke up. "Your dad is going to be mad at us if we chase them down and bring them back because we went where we weren't supposed to be. But I'm thinking he'd be even more mad at us if we left them alone and they got lost or hurt or something. I think we need to go after them and bring them back."

Maryann, Melissa, and Kathy agreed. Kathy said, "Suzie was the one who started all the stuff in the barn about Maryann. What goes on in her head anyway? This is dumb with a capital D. We're all going to be in trouble, but I'd rather we stuck together."

Todd turned Desperado around and cued him to canter with the others following him. They had some ground to make up. Suzie and Heidi were almost out of sight ahead of them.

It was still a couple of hours before they had to be back at the ranch. They hurried to catch up with the miscreants. Nobody had much to say as they cantered along the trail. They were so engrossed in what they were doing they didn't see all the wildlife around them or the first signs of the wildfire in the forest. They missed the badger on the hillside. They didn't see the gray squirrels rushing up the bark of trees to get out of their way. They didn't see the dark blue mountain jays flitting from tree to tree. They didn't see the hawk catch a thermal and ride it high above them looking for a meal of rabbit, squirrel or a deer mouse to snack on. When they passed the ranch, they were far enough away no one from the ranch saw them.

CHAPTER THREE

Three Years Earlier

Henry Babcock thought he had a lead on just the right property. Savannah, his wife, wanted a Ski Chalet for entertaining a few miles north of Boulder, Colorado. She'd taken a drive from Denver to Wyoming once and fell in love with the countryside. She wanted a property not too far from Boulder for the convenience, but she wanted the chalet to be out in the country with a view of the mountains. She thought it would be nice to take friends there during the spring and summers as an alternative to the Villa in Tuscany.

He found a beautiful 40-acre property that had been a working horse ranch. He discovered the owner passed away recently and left the property to his nearly 80-year old wife. He thought, with the right incentive, she might be willing to sell the property to him and move to town. Anyone in their right mind could see 40 acres of property would be too much for one little old woman to manage by herself.

Henry flew into Denver and rented a car. He'd seen photos of the property taken by a land specialist who worked for him. He needed to see it for himself and maybe get a chance to talk to the widow. He looked around Boulder as he drove through with some interest. It was the University town in Northern Colorado and it offered cultural events his wife would love. He didn't expect to spend too much time there, just use the chalet for vacation time on occasion.

Henry wanted to see the view of the mountains before talking to the widow. He parked off the road a way back from her driveway. He walked around near the road until he found a trail heading into the woods alongside the property. He walked down the trail looking around at the view. He noted the outbuildings, barns, and sheds on the back portion of the property. The fact large trees had been taken out to provide turnouts and arenas for the horses only made the property more attractive to him. Barns and sheds were easy to take down. The open space created better views of the mountains without him having to remove the trees himself. He also saw a partial view of the main house. It wasn't very big and would come down easily to provide space for his wife's chalet. A couple of days work with a dozer would prepare the land perfectly for what he had in mind. Money was no object for him. There was a little stream running through the property too. The original owner built a stout bridge crossing it along this trail. It was obvious the trail had been used for riding horses. The more he saw, the more he liked it and thought about what he needed to do to get it and start his own building project.

Desperado was nearly three years old and used his sneaky tricks to escape his stall whenever he wanted to. He'd eaten his breakfast in the stall next to his mother and picked the lock Hilda closed after feeding and watering horses that morning. He took off down the trail in the woods looking for the deer again. He learned a lot from them. He knew what was safe to eat, where it was safe to travel and what to avoid in the woods. That particular day he had a funny feeling that something was not quite right. He was looking for one special doe that he often talked to about things. She was a lovely little thing, slight and delicate looking with a tail that flagged like his own. Hers was much smaller, of course, and the underside of her tail was covered with short white hairs which made her a member of the White Tail Deer Clan. When they bounded away from danger, they flagged their tails naturally and the white underside showed.

Desperado didn't find the doe that morning. He thought she must be off with the rest of the does and their fawns. He turned around and sauntered down the trail toward home. He was bored but stopped to nibble on interesting bits of grass along the trail until he heard something on the trail ahead of him. He paused and sniffed the air, pricking his ears forward. There was someone on the trail he didn't recognize. He stepped off the trail into the woods and watched for a few minutes. The man was going back toward the road and had not seen him. He didn't belong here. Desperado stood very still and kept his eye on the stranger. A bunny hopped out of the woods onto the trail in front of the man. The man kicked at him!

Desperado was incensed. Nobody kicked at bunnies. He was so much bigger than that poor little bunny. That bunny lived here. The man did not, in fact, he was not supposed to be here at all. Desperado rushed onto the trail and headed for the man. The man heard the hooves pounding on the trail and turned around, saw Desperado coming and began to run toward the road. He tripped over a root in the trail and fell hard. He was trying to get back on his feet when Desperado reached him and launched himself into the air. Desperado jumped over the man and spun around. He pulled his front legs off the ground and stood on his hind legs and screamed at the man. The man scrabbled in the dirt, turned himself around so his butt was on the trail and he pushed himself off the trail with his feet and hands until his back came up against a tree trunk. He quickly pulled himself up and rushed behind the tree using it as a shield between him and Desperado.

Desperado saw the fear in the man's eyes. He was satisfied with that. He was sure the poor little bunny looked at the man the same way the man was now looking at him. He dropped back down on four legs and shook himself. He also realized Hilda had probably heard him so she knew he was out of his stall again and would be looking for him. He trotted down the trail again, looking over his shoulder at the man a couple of times until he reached the bend in the trail and lost sight of him. He was satisfied with himself. He was pretty sure that man would never kick at a bunny again.

Henry was madder than mad. Nothing ever dared attacked him! He wanted that horse! He would make him pay for what he did if it was the last thing he ever did. He brushed off his clothing and walked back to the road. He walked up the driveway to the main house and knocked on the door.

Hilda had few visitors, and nobody ever dropped in without calling her first. She peeked through the lace curtain in her living room and saw a portly middle-aged man standing at the door. She didn't recognize him. She left the chain lock on the door and opened it a crack to see what he wanted.

"Yes, may I help you?" she asked.

"I'm looking for Mrs. Jorgensen. Is she here?" the man asked.

"I'm Mrs. Jorgensen," she answered.

"My name is Henry Babcock, ma'am. I'd like to talk to you about your ranch if you have a minute. And there's a loose horse prowling around. Wouldn't be one of yours, would it? He's quite handsome."

Hilda looked the man over through the crack in the door and decided he couldn't be a mass murderer. He just didn't have the right look for that in her mind. She slipped the chain off the door and opened it wider. "That must be Desperado. He's our escape artist. Don't know how he does it but he can pick any lock you put on his stall. He's just a two-year-old so he's like a teenaged boy. He likes to wander around a bit. I'll collect him in a few minutes. What exactly did you want to know about my ranch?"

"Actually, Mrs. Jorgensen, I heard you are a recent widow, God rest his soul, and thought you might be interested in selling the place. I know 40 acres is a lot of property to maintain and thought it be more than you want to tackle all by yourself," Henry explained.

Hilda was shocked. How did that fat little man know anything about her Jan passing away? Who was he anyway? And how did he know Desperado was out of his stall if he hadn't been snooping around where he didn't belong. Suddenly Hilda's red flag went up and she was angry. Hilda's voice raised as her anger level grew.

"Just who do you think you are? How do you know anything about me and my Jan? Why are you snooping around on my property? This is private property. I own it free and clear and the taxes are paid up. Now get off my land and don't come back! Do you hear me?" By that time Hilda was screaming. "Get off my land! Get off my property NOW!"

Desperado heard Hilda screaming at the man. She was furious and possibly a tiny bit afraid. He thought he heard a tinge of fear in her voice. He ran for the house at full speed. If the bunny kicker man was hurting his Hilda, he'd be sorry!

Henry Babcock hurried down the driveway to the road and was almost at his car when Desperado rushed up from behind him. He barely got inside the car and slammed the door when Desperado flew past. Desperado turned to face the man through the windshield of his car. He realized he was not going to be able to get at the man with the car in the way so he turned around and kicked the front of the car with both hind feet. He kicked hard. The hood crumpled and the windshield cracked. The man desperately poked the key in the ignition and started the car as Desperado kicked the front of the car once more. The left headlight exploded and the grill crushed into the radiator. The man put the car in gear and stepped on the gas. Desperado hopped sideways, out of the way and let the car pass with one last kick into the rear quarter panel. The tail light on the driver's side flew in chunks onto the highway behind the car. Hilda was running toward him.

Hilda caught up with Desperado and threw her arms around his neck sobbing. "You could have been killed you big lug! What would I do without you? Come on now, I have some treats for you in the barn. Thanks for coming to my rescue. I'm sure that bad old Henry Babcock will never set foot around here again!" She held onto a small piece of Desperado's mane and led him back to the barn. She took a few minutes to give him a good brushing while she got her own emotions under control. Hilda had gone from curiosity to shock, then anger and finally fear in a few short minutes. That was enough emotion for anyone in a single day much less a few minutes. She was a little shaky. She talked to Desperado as she brushed.

"I think you need to go back to Cold Water Creek Ranch for a while. You need to learn a few things and you're getting to be such a big boy. Chris will teach you what Jan can't. You'll be right down the street so I can come see you every day. I know you like it there. You love learning new things and maybe you won't get yourself in so much trouble. What do you think?"

Brushing the horse calmed Hilda as it always did. The more she brushed the steadier she became. By the time Desperado's deep bay coat gleamed, Hilda was back to her normal self. "You sure put the fear of God into the fat little man, didn't you?" she chuckled. "I don't think he'll be back here." Hilda walked Desperado into his stall and measured out a nice portion of his favorite grain and added a couple of apples to top it off with when she put it all into his feeder. "Thanks for coming to my rescue, young man. That was pretty daring of you and I love you even more," she told him. Hilda added hay in his stall and fed his mother before going back to the house for the night.

Desperado thought about the bunny-kicker man. He had a name. Hilda called him Henry Babcock. There was something about him that made Desperado very uneasy. He didn't like him at all. He hoped he would never see that man again.

Henry Babcock got a mile and a half down the highway before his rental car stopped running. The crack in the radiator leaked all the radiator fluid out of the car and poured over the hot engine so it steamed under the hood. He was madder than a wet hen. That horse was going to pay for this, one way or another. He'd make sure of it. He stewed on that while he waited for a tow truck to haul the car back to the rental yard in Boulder. He took another rental to the airport in Denver and flew back to San Francisco. He was still shaking with rage when he got off the plane. He stopped at his office and made several phone calls before going home for the night. Mrs. Jorgensen called the horse Desperado. He had a name. They would find him. He would buy him, whatever it took. That horse would pay for what he did. He'd be very sorry he ever messed with Henry Babcock!

Two weeks earlier...

Henry Babcock was livid. He had enough money to buy every one of those bureaucrats in Boulder ten times over, and still they put roadblocks in his path! He was a man that never took "NO" for an answer. He wanted those darned trees gone. They were in his way. He was throwing a fit of epic proportions. Things flew off his deck as he slammed his fists down in rage.

Henry was a businessman who struggled from childhood poverty in the Eastern European slums of New York City. He put himself through school and worked in restaurants washing dishes and mopping floors and doing jobs no one else wanted. His mother, in her dowdy house dress and babushka, worked as a maid to help him. He got himself hired by a Wall Street brokerage firm and worked day and night to make his first million. He plundered other brokers accounts and did whatever it took to make money. He remained single because he didn't have the time or inclination to find himself a wife. He decided he didn't need the distraction of one anyway.

That was before he met Savannah Hooper. He was attending a fundraiser for a good cause in a five-star hotel in San Francisco and went more to mingle and make business connections than stand for the cause. He was smitten clear across the room by the loveliest creature he'd ever laid his eyes on. Like everything else in his life, he refused to take "NO" for an answer and married her within six months. It didn't matter to him that he was short, balding and paunchy around the middle. When the beautiful Savannah got wind of the size of his bank account, it didn't bother her either.

She taught him the fine art of developing connections through entertaining. He bought her a large penthouse in New York City, a lovely compound along the lakeshore outside of Chicago, a large flat in London and a beautiful villa in Tuscany. Her current wish list included a place in Colorado to bring friends during the ski season and occasional summer retreats. He found a nice 20-acre property. There was one property between his and Cold Water Creek Ranch to the south and one property between his and the Jorgensen place to the north. He lucked out and found an older couple wanting to retire to Florida. He paid cash for it. He had his architect draw up plans for a 20,000 square foot ski lodge on three levels. It included opulent rooms for guests, a huge game room for the gentlemen, a large open kitchen and living room, and large partially covered decks to take advantage of the view. Savannah had been to the property and wanted a bridge built over the brook which ran slightly away from the outdoor deck area. She wanted a small deck built on the other side of the bridge to take advantage of the sunshine during the summer.

He had nothing but trouble getting his plans approved in the first place. His architect had to make change after change to satisfy the planning department in Boulder. When he added the bridge and small deck on the other side of the main outdoor deck, they turned him down flat. In order to build that, he would have to cut down a small stand of two-hundred-year-old Cottonwood trees that grew beside the brook. They were protected by law. He could not cut them down; therefore he could not build his bridge and deck where he wanted them.

He'd also had nothing but trouble with the contractors. Either they didn't show up when they were supposed to or they did and made changes that were not approved by the inspectors or him. The entire project had been nothing but a trial.

The last straw was the refusal of the planning department to let him remove the trees that were in his way. He would fix that once and for all if it took every penny he had. He made one call. "Do you know who I am?" he asked the man who answered the phone. "Well, then, we understand each other. I need a job done as soon as possible. I will send you the specifications for the job and an extra package for your trouble. Is there anything else you need from me?" Henry nodded his head as he hung up the phone. He called his secretary in and gave her a package to over-night to Denver for him, closed his office and went home without another thought about his problem. It was taken care of as far as he was concerned.

On his way down in the elevator, he thought about it for a while. Colorado had not been one of his favorite places. First, there was the darned rabbit that jumped in front of him and almost scared him to death in the woods. It was just so unexpected is all. The rabbit didn't frighten him, it was just the surprise, he conceded. Then that horrible horse tried to run him down. Then his very polite conversation with an 80-year-old woman ended in her screaming at him and the horse trying to attack him again. He was stuck on the highway for two hours because of the damage that horse did to his rental car. He wanted his revenge against that horse.

He'd tried through several agents to buy it and, no matter how much he offered for it, the old woman turned him down. The horse was not for sale.

It took a while, but one of his people dug up her son's phone number. He called him personally and offered up to six figures for the horse. The son had no interest in the horse himself but couldn't talk his mom into selling him. He tried calling her daughter as well and they had a nice long conversation. She wanted her mother to move in with her and sell the whole ranch but she refused. She couldn't live in a two-story house with college kids running in and out at all hours. Hilda Jorgensen was perfectly healthy so there was nothing her children could do until she passed away or got sick enough to be put in a home. But they both saw the dollar signs every time they visited their mother and she dragged them down to the ranch to see her Desperado. Both of them kept Henry Babcock's private number close at hand.

Henry Babcock knew he would exact his revenge. It was just a matter of time. He'd try to be patient.

CHAPTER FOUR

As soon as the riders left the ranch, the ladies went back to the house to clean up the kitchen, have another cup of coffee or tea and sit in the living room visiting. They laughed as they told each other stories about their children and their husbands. The men finished up the ranch tour and sat relaxing on the back patio to enjoy the view. In was beautiful in Colorado that time of year. The sun was shining and the air was a balmy seventy-eight degrees. White fluffy clouds formed over the tops of the mountain peaks to the west changing shape with each passing moment. The shade of the patio was comfortable. The meadow beyond the ranch was green and peppered with wildflowers. The mountains in the distance took on a blueish hue while the closer ones appeared green and glorious. Younger children played with one of Todd's soccer balls in the grass beyond the patio or amused themselves playing Todd's video games in the playroom off the kitchen.

A stiff breeze blew up from the south a little before noon. It began to blow hard and those outside came in to get out of the wind. The first sign of trouble to come was the sirens along the highway when the first Forestry Service trucks went charging into battle with a rapidly spreading fire. The wind was gusty now and blowing hard to the north. Chris and Sharon heard the sirens and went outside to look. They saw nothing south or west of the ranch and walked up the driveway to the highway. That's when they saw the large cloud of black smoke blown by the winds. It was north of them, but not very far. As they watched in disbelief, they saw the fire jump the highway and begin burning on the west side. Soon a long line of red fire trucks came blasting down the highway heading north. There was a large development of homes east of the highway in that direction. These brave men and women were going to try and get ahead of the fire and set up structure protection for that development. Evacuees began streaming south along the highway. Chris heard the first helicopter in the air as the clouds of black smoke grew larger and thicker.

Chris looked at Sharon and said, "I'd better ride out and get the kids back here. I don't think it's a good idea for them to be out in the woods with all this going on." He turned and headed for the barn. Chris took his personal riding horse out of the stall and saddled him quickly. He walked out of the barn and galloped him to the back fence of the property. He leaned over and opened the gate and kept on riding as quickly as he could for the meadow where the kids were going for their ride and lunch.

Chris's heart stopped when he reached the meadow and found it empty. He could see where the kids had been and where the horses were tied between trees. Rocks along the bank of the stream were still wet above the water line which told him they had not been gone long. He looked around and found their tracks. Following the trail of hoof prints and road apples, he realized they were heading north. That was exactly what he didn't want to find. He followed their tracks until they disappeared in the burning brush left behind by the fire. He was choking from the smoke. The heat was getting to his horse. Ash and burning embers covered everything. He followed the trail until he couldn't continue without harming himself or his horse. The winds were whipping ash in the air so much it was difficult for him to breath. His eyes and the eyes of his horse were streaming tears from the smoke. He could see the active fire to the north. He was beside himself. He turned his horse around and rode home as fast as possible. He'd told those kids to go only where they said they were going. They ignored his instructions. Now they were in danger of a raging fire behind them and no way to get back home! He prayed they were able to outrun the fire on horseback. He was sick to think maybe they couldn't.

Chris hollered for Sharon as he galloped past the house for the barn. She rushed out as he untacked his horse. He was angry and he was scared. He had no idea what to do.

Shaking, Chris told Sharon what he'd found. Sharon was panicked. "What are we going to do?" she asked. "We'd better call Hilda Jorgensen. Her ranch is right in the path of that fire. She doesn't drive. She needs to get out of there. I think we need to call the Fire Department and let them know the kids are out in that and about Hilda too. Hilda needs help to evacuate and we can't get there from here."

Sharon rushed to her office in the barn to make the calls, thankful for something to do. Chris went back to the house to break the news to the families there.

Sharon returned to the house a few minutes later. She told Chris that Hilda did not answer her phone. All they could do was pray Hilda found a ride out. She told the Fire Department about the nine riders who were probably in the path of the fire, explaining they were all thirteen and fourteen years old and on horseback. She gave the phone numbers for the barn, the house, and both cell phone numbers to contact if they located the kids. She let them know the parents of the riders were at Cold Water Creek Ranch with them waiting for news.

The mood in the room was somber as the news settled in. There were nine kids out there in the path of a major fire and there was not one thing they could do but sit and wait for news. Several mothers broke down. They were comforted by their husbands. After a while, things got quiet. The adults didn't have much to say. The younger kids played quietly in the playroom. They knew something was wrong but not what. They sensed the mood of the adults and stayed together out of the way. No one left the ranch that night. None of the parents got much sleep.

Henry Babcock was in his penthouse office in San Francisco and turned on the television to the ABC affiliate for the early news broadcast about 4:00 p.m. that afternoon. He wanted to catch the commuter traffic report. He had a date with his wife at the Met that night at 8:00 p.m. and needed to know how long it would take to get home so he could shower and change. He was stunned when the broadcast covered a forest fire just north of Boulder, Colorado during the broadcast. It showed some aerial shots that looked like it could be near his land in Colorado. He made some phone calls. He was further alarmed when he heard it was his land in Colorado and might have been the place where the fire originated. The TV newscaster reported it as a major fire engulfing acres of land, homes, ranches, and wildland with no end in sight and, more importantly, it was a suspected arson case. He tried to reach the number he had in Denver and got no answer. He tried several more times on his way home to no avail. He excused himself from the production at the Met several times to call the number in Denver with no result. Besides having to explain away his absences to his lovely wife, he was irritated by the nonresponsiveness of the man he hired. He made several more calls and the people promised to report to him in the morning. All he could do was wait.

CHAPTER FIVE

Just as the nine riders passed Cold Water Creek Ranch heading north, a new red Corvette pulled into the driveway at the construction site a quarter of a mile north of the ranch. A man stepped out of the car and looked around, seeing a group of large cottonwood trees across the brook from the building site. He noticed the framing for a three-story structure was almost complete. The interior walls were framed but the plumbing and electrical work were not yet finished. He saw a staked area close to the trees on the other side of the brook. "That must be it," he thought to himself. He noticed orange ribbons around the lower branches of four of the cottonwood trees. They were the ones in the way of the staked area. It was obvious where his work needed to be done.

The man began pulling items from the trunk of the car and stacked them on the driveway. There was little traffic along the highway and his car was screened by the construction, so he wasn't too worried about being seen. He pulled four thick paper canisters out of the trunk and punctured a hole in the bottom of each one. In doing that, he accidentally cut his thumb on his knife. He didn't notice the three drops of blood that dripped onto the driveway while he worked. He pushed a fuse through the bottom of each canister, filling the hole he punched in it. He sat the canisters on the driveway and pulled out a container of a dry chemical compound he'd perfected for his special purpose. He filled each paper canister with the dry powdery substance, put a lid on each one and tucked them into a pouch slung around his neck. He would be doing his work on the side of the trees away from the highway. A stiff breeze blew across the site scattering leaves and debris. The breeze dissipated a little. The breeze came and went as the man put his devices together. He walked toward the trees until he came to the edge of the brook. The man had to either wade across the brook or attempt to jump over it. He looked at his shoes and shook his head. Either way, they were going to get wet. He rolled up his pants legs and waded, carrying his tools with him. He heard a few cars pass by on the highway, but he wasn't visible behind the massive trunks of the trees as he worked. The breeze increased in intensity while he worked. He thought he should have checked on the weather for this afternoon, but put that thought out of his mind when he remembered the size of the package that was delivered to him that day. All he had to do was burn these four trees and he could enjoy a nice vacation in the Bahamas.

The man used a lawn rake to push dead leaves and debris in a deep layer on the ground around the base of the trees. He used a staple gun to attach the paper containers to the trees themselves and adjusted the fuses to extend down to the level of the debris. He flicked his lighter and touched the first fuse. It sparked to life and gave off a puff of smoke as the fuse burned upward toward his homemade incendiary device. He flicked his lighter three more times and saw three more fuses begin to burn. The fuse on the first tree dropped sparks down into the leave pile at the base of the tree. It began smoldering.

By the time he'd lit all four fuses, the breeze strengthened into a strong wind blowing 40 miles per hour from the south as a cold front moved into the area along the eastern edge of the mountains. A low-pressure system from the west forced the high-pressure system over the area to move north. The front created winds that blew northward and grew in strength and intensity rather quickly. As the man watched, one of his devices blow off the tree and landed in the leaf pile at the base. It exploded in flames. The wind blew blazing leaves around which started other spot fires. He watched in a weird fascination as embers drifted into the framing of the mansion across the brook. The wind fanned the flames by the trees into the wooden framework. Very quickly the small fire became a raging inferno. The wood framing provided an excellent source of dry fuel. The wind increased available oxygen to the fire and it began to devour everything in its path. Once the flames reached the third floor of the mansion, embers were blown into the crowns of the tall pines close by. The ground fires were spreading at the same time and caught the lower branches of those same trees. The 40-foot trees became candles burning from bottom to top spreading flames to neighboring trees and shooting flames 50 feet high in the air above them.

The man realized he'd made a complete mess of this job. This wasn't something he'd expected. He was used to setting fires inside of buildings or vehicles, not out in the open. He forgot about his shoes and his pant legs and ran through the brook, tossed his tools in the trunk, slammed the trunk shut and climbed into the Corvette. He backed out of the driveway. He turned onto the highway and put the pedal to the metal. He didn't see one of the other incendiary devices blew off the tree he attached it to. It fell in the brook. The water extinguished it and swept it downstream. It snagged on rocks close to the surface a few feet from where it entered the water. The flow of the water was not strong enough to dislodge it.

The man had to get out of the area as quickly as possible. He headed for Boulder and that fancy hotel restaurant and bar where he'd left his date for the weekend while he did a "little business" outside of town. From the look on his face when he showed up to get her, she didn't argue when he told her they had to get back to Denver. She didn't ask him about his wet pants and shoes. She didn't ask him about the soot on his clothes and his hands. During the drive, the man reached his travel agent by phone and had two seats booked on a flight through Miami to the Bahamas. He got back to his townhouse and packed a suitcase before driving his friend to her apartment so she could pack one too. They were on a flight out of the country within hours.

CHAPTER SIX

The first call on the fire came into the Fire Dispatch Center minutes after the red Corvette pulled out on the highway heading for Boulder. By the time the first responders arrived, the winds were blowing forty miles an hour due north and the structure of the mansion was in ruins. Most of the framework had fallen in on the foundation, still smoldering and burning here and there. The four cottonwood trees were scorched. One had significant burning up the south side of the tree but all of them would probably survive the fire. The rest of the forest was in trouble. Fire burning up the trunks of the pines crowned, sending flames and embers into neighboring treetops. Ground fires were spreading north at a rapid pace, enveloping shrubs and grasses and lighting the bottoms of the tall trees and the shorter aspens in their way.

The first responders immediately called in to report their findings and ask for more help. "Chief, this fire could burn all the way to Wyoming at the rate it's going. We need everything we can get on it. We need air support as soon as possible. We're going to need ground crews too. There are a number of properties on the west side of the highway that need to be evacuated and there's a pretty large development about six or seven miles north of ground zero on the east side of the highway we need to lay in structure protection for. With the way this fire is crowning, it won't take long before it crosses the highway and begins to burn on the east side too. This has all the earmarks of a major rager!"

The first crew at the burned out construction site spotted the incendiary device locations on the cottonwood trees. This fire was intentionally set! They cordoned off the area with yellow tape to keep everyone out until the arson investigators got there. One of them called in his report on the probable arson so the Fire Chief could get investigators on board right away.

Planes rushed off runways and lumbered skyward hauling thousands of pounds of water and fire retardant. Helicopters pulled giant buckets of water under their bellies as well. After reports from the air, the Fire Chief added crews with bulldozers to build and expand fire breaks ahead of the fire. The dozers plowed down everything in their path, including 40 and 50 feet tall trees. They widened the firebreaks already in the forest because of the wind blowing the fire from crown to crown among the tallest trees. Ground crew with shovels and pickaxes worked alongside the dozers leaving bare earth in wide swatches that would give the fire nothing to burn.

The Highway Patrol personnel went from property to property north of the fire calling for mandatory evacuations of properties in its path. Evacuees took what they could and rushed out on the highway southward toward Boulder. Horse and Livestock trailers began turning in to Cold Water Creek Ranch looking for sanctuary for their horses and livestock because it was the closest place in a safety zone. Many people needed to make multiple trips. Everyone at the ranch pitched in with evacuated stock. They set up extra water, feed, and helped reassure the owners they'd watch over their animals. In one way the evacuations helped the Cold Water Creek Ranch crew more than anything else. It gave them something immediate and physical to do while they waited for word about their kids. They weren't just sitting around and worrying.

Chris and Sharon directed everyone, told where the extra water buckets and feed buckets were kept, where to put the newcomers and where to park trailers so others had room to maneuver coming and going. It was a madhouse for a while. It didn't take long to fill every vacant barn stall. They used turnouts, round pens, outdoor arenas and the covered arena for horses. They had several six-foot welded wire enclosures for stallions that worked for goats and dogs. Evacuated owners stayed to make sure their animals were settled in before leaving for town and sanctuary for themselves. The women from Cold Water Creek Ranch kept coffee, ice tea and bottles of water at the ready for visitors.

When the fire crossed the highway and began burning on both sides, few people traveled the highway south to Boulder. Many were forced to drive north toward Wyoming for safety. Soon the only vehicles passing Cold Water Creek Ranch were fire vehicles with flashing lights.

The Fire Chief, Don Odom, stopped and asked if he could use a portion of the property for his Command and Control unit. He and his assistants needed to be close to the action not twenty miles away in Boulder. Don knew Chris and Sharon O'Neal personally. His daughter had the riding bug and took lessons from Chris for years. They boarded her horse with the O'Neal's. When she went off to college, his wife took care of her horse and started taking lessons herself. The Odoms were at the ranch frequently. Chris and Sharon had no problem hosting the Fire Chief. Chris helped spot the large RV close to the highway and showed the fire people where they could park their other vehicles.

Things at Cold Water Creek Ranch got even crazier when the Fire Crews inhabited part of the ranch. It gave the women more to do. They kept up a non-stop running stream of hot coffee for the crews working until they were exhausted. The coffee helped keep their adrenaline levels high for the task at hand.

Cell towers alongside the highway burned as easily as 50-foot trees. Radios on units needed to ping off the towers to maintain communications with central command. Radios lost their effectiveness when the towers burned so they all turned to satellite phone technology. Communications become a complicated mess when smoke from the fire affected even that.

The ranch just south of Cold Water Creek Ranch became the central point for ground and engine crews to swap out exhausted men and pick up additional equipment. Pop-up shelters went up in rows to provide shade for men taking breaks from the action and for those waiting their turn fighting the beast. Portable grills turned out high-quality protein meals for hungry firefighters.

Chief Odom sent engine crews to the large development north of the fire for structure protection. Those men and women would stand with their backs to homes of people they didn't know using high-pressure water hoses to keep the flames from burning them down. The inhabitants fled north with what little they could carry leaving unnamed men behind to protect their homes and their dreams.

Fire crews stopped at properties on the west side of the highway and attempted to keep the flames from the homes there. For some they were successful, for others they arrived too late. When they arrived at Hilda Jorgensen's ranch, the barn was completely engulfed. There was no saving it. Two of the storage sheds on the property were also too far gone to save. They made a herculean effort to save her home. Once the burning embers found a place to burn on the underside of the eaves, there was no saving it. They doused the home for as long as they could safely, then had to turn tail and run to save their own lives. Several of the fighters shed tears as they drove away. They hated to lose.

Each section of forest and each home the firefighters worked to save was personal to them. Every home lost became a symbol of their own home and they felt the loss almost as deeply as they would have if it had been their own. They gave up when the only option was their own death as a sacrifice for it. They had to live so they could continue the fight.

The fight went on hour after hour, tree by tree, acre by acre through the night. The winds slowed down after sundown, but the fire refused to lie down. The crowning, or treetop to treetop spread, continued for miles, jumping over fire retardant paths and fanning out in new directions to the north, west, and east as dry fuel maintained it.

CHAPTER SEVEN

The wind pushed the flames from the construction site northward. It ate everything combustible in its path. The dryness caused by the drought made things a lot worse. Dry piles of leaves and shrubs exploded in flames the minute embers landed in them.

The kids and horses were only a half mile north of the construction site when the blaze broke out. At first, they had no idea there was trouble behind them. The first few drifts of smoke in the air were chalked off to someone's barbecue. There were a few nice homes close to the road west of them. All too soon the smoke and ash began to over-power them. The kids and the horses were choking on the smoke. Other forest animals began to flee the area. The sound of the fire behind them began to roar like a freight train, scaring them even more. Sounds of toppling trees crashing down didn't help either. Ash and embers rained down on them, stinging their skin and the horses. The smoke was so thick they could hardly see and their eyes began tearing and burning.

Tears streamed from Desperado's eyes, ran down his muzzle and dripped to the ground as he picked his way through the forest. His vision blurred by his tears and the smoke and ash in the air. His heart pounded with an adrenalin rush. He *must* keep moving forward if he was to get the others to safety. Other forest creatures rushing away from the inferno behind them streaked between his legs nearly tripping him at times. He ignored them as they ignored him. They were in full flight mode.

The kids were startled when a large cougar streaked by them. Hot on her heels were her two young kittens the size of 50-pound dogs. They saw and ignored bunnies, squirrels, and ground rodents but glanced fearfully when the larger animals came bounding by. One buck mule deer with a large rack bounced ahead of them and ran smack into a tree. The impact stunned the deer and he fell to the ground. The kids watched in surprise as he lifted his head and shook himself. He jumped up and bounded onward like a kangaroo jumping over low bushes and shrubs. They were fearful when the black bear and her squalling cub ran by them within two feet of the horses' legs. She completely ignored them. They were amazed at how fast she traveled for her bulky size. She slowed a bit to let her cub catch up before disappearing into the haze.

Desperado made a sudden turn to the east, almost unseating Todd. Todd had given up trying to guide Desperado but picked the reins up to turn him north again when he realized where Desperado was going. Todd hung onto the saddle horn with one hand to steady himself and he signaled the others about the turn.

Desperado was going to the Jorgenson farm. He knew this area like the front of his hoof. He'd been born here six years ago. Jan and Hilda Jorgenson lived on this property for forty years breeding Arabian horses. Desperado was the last one they bred before Jan passed away. He was over eighty when he died. Desperado was the finest horse they'd ever bred. He did have some interesting quirks that drove Jan crazy at times. He was a notorious escape artist.

Desperado loved to explore the territory around the farm. Fortunately, that experience would help him now.

Desperado heard Hilda's children discussing the sale of him and his mother to Henry Babcock, the bunny-kicker man, on their infrequent visits to the barn with Hilda in the past few months. They only talked about it when Hilda was not close enough to hear them. They were waiting until Hilda passed away or got sick enough for them to put her in a place they called a "rest home," whatever that was. He didn't want to be sold to the bunny-kicker man. He'd seen the rage on the man's face through the windshield of the car after he'd kicked it. He didn't like the bunny-kicker man at all and the thought of being sold to him and giving him a position of power over Indent for new paragraph frightened him. But Desperado also truly loved Hilda and would do anything to protect her.

Desperado led the other eight horses straight to Hilda's back door. Todd jumped out of the saddle and stood banging furiously on the door. Hilda was in her living room with her back to the window so she didn't notice the light dim because of the smoke. Hilda dropped the book she was reading and hurried through the kitchen to the back door before she saw and smelled the smoke in the air.

When she opened the door, Todd said, "Come on Hilda, we've got to go! I'll give you a boost up on Desperado and ride behind you. Do you think you can hang on?"

Hilda took one look to the south and grabbed the doorframe for support in her shock. She held on for a second, then let go and looked into Todd's pleading face. "Yes, give me a hand up. I can hold on just fine. Let's get out of here! Please stop by the barn so we can let Desperado's mother out."

Todd boosted Hilda into the saddle and scrambled on the back. Before he had a chance to pick up the reins, Desperado turned and led the group through the front entrance of the breezeway barn. Brody jumped down and handed his reins to Becky while he unlatched the stall door for Annabella, Desperado's mother. She was beside herself at that moment, locked in the barn smelling the smoke. She was terrified and wanted to run.

Desperado squealed to her *"Mom, stay with us. Follow me. I know a place to go where we will be safe, but we have to hurry!"* He headed back into the forest in a northwesterly direction. He screamed over his shoulder to Prince Ali, *"Ali please stay at the rear and keep the rest of the horses bunched together. I know a safe place. Follow me!"*

Todd held Hilda with one hand and the saddle horn with the other. When Hilda looked south from her back door, she could see the flames were on both sides of the highway and the head of the fire wasn't too far south of them. They had to move or burn and they couldn't go east or south. She covered her nose with the loose sweater she was wearing and closed her eyes.

All ten horses picked their way through the forest quickly as they tried to stay in clear areas. The only one of the group who'd ever jumped a horse was Heidi. She and Schultzy had never jumped more than 2'6" and some of the obstacles in the forest were higher. She didn't want to try jumping in these conditions anyway. Prince Ali took up the drag position at the back of the group to keep stragglers moving. He tucked his tail to keep the embers from stinging his behind. Charlie, Becky, and Todd were the only ones who'd ridden in the area before. Charlie stayed in the middle to help the kids from California who were completely out of their element and scared to death. The girls pulled their tee-shirts up over their noses to help themselves breathe through the smoke and ash. The boys resorted to their tee-shirts too. The exertion caused the horses to cough and gag as the smoke enveloped them all.

About three miles northwest of Hilda's ranch, Desperado made a sudden turn west. He continued moving in that direction for quite a while. The air became clearer the farther west they traveled. He found the deer trail he was looking for. One of the mountains got closer and closer as the group picked their way along the tiny trail. He led the group to the bottom of a tall flat faced cliff and paralleled the rock wall a short distance. Desperado suddenly turned into the rock wall and walked through an opening you wouldn't have seen if you weren't right on it. It was offset and slanted and several yards deep. Desperado led the group through the mouth of a canyon. The canyon widened out several yards from the opening. It was about a mile deep, about a quarter mile wide at most and sloped upward a hundred and fifty feet or more. Sometime in the past, a tremor loosened rock along the ridgeline. Rocks tumbled down into the canyon taking all the brush and trees that grew on the sides of the canyon to the bottom and buried them. Jagged walls with rock piles at the bottom were all that was left behind. There was nothing left to burn except for the grass that grew around the edges of a pool at the apex. Near the top of the canyon was a natural spring. The rockfall opened the spring. Water slowly tumbled down the rocks and into a slight depression in the ground at the apex of the canyon. It formed a pool of clear water about four feet deep.

The air inside the canyon was clear. The smoke passed by the opening and the mountain blocked it from this isolated little space. Once the group reached the pool, everyone dismounted and let the horses have a much-needed drink. They stood around numbed by the experience. Everyone checked their horses and Annabella, Desperado's mother. The kids were relieved when the horses' eyes stopped tearing and they stopped coughing. About every half an hour one of them walked back to the rocky opening and looked out to see what they could of the forest beyond. For a while, all they could see was smoke and ash in the distance. After a couple of hours, they could see the fire coming in their direction. Fortunately, there was no brush to burn near the opening of the canyon. The fire turned north and found more fuel before burning around them to the west.

Only three of the kids still had their cell phones. The others were lost in the rush to get away from the fire. They tried to get a signal on the phones but couldn't. There was no signal in this remote location. There was no way to call anyone and let them know they were okay. There was no way they could call and let anyone know where they were. Hours dragged on. As the sun dropped on the horizon, the kids went through their packs and found a couple of packages of crackers and a couple of bags of chips. There was nothing else to eat. Hilda pulled out a scarf and put all the food on it so it could be divided up among the ten people stranded. They ate a meager meal, drank some of the spring water from the pond with their hands as cups and waited. The temperature in the canyon dropped when the sun set. The kids wore only shorts or jeans and tee-shirts. That day started out sunny and seventy-eight degrees. They lay in the grass beside the pond and huddled together shivering, using the nine saddle pads for cover. They hoped for rescue in the morning. All ten spent a terrible night in complete darkness on the cold rocky ground.

CHAPTER EIGHT

As dawn broke the next morning a large male cougar crept through the entrance to the canyon on scorched pads. He'd smelled water. Once inside the canyon, he smelled something else more inviting. He kept to the wall and stalked toward the horses. They were large but he'd downed a bull elk before and knew one of them would feed him for more than a week.

Desperado spotted the large cat. He nosed Prince Ali awake. *"Take a look over there, will you,"* he said to Ali.

Ali's heart began to thump in his chest. *"I had one of those jump on me before. They have big teeth and long claws. I have the scars to prove it too. I think he's looking to eat one of us.*

"How about we teach him a lesson," Desperado said under his breath. He just couldn't let that cat harm Hilda, Todd or any of the others. He'd thought about it before waking Ali.

"What did you have in mind?" Ali asked nervously.

"He can't catch two of us at the same time. I think we need to charge him. I'll bet he runs away if he thinks we are going to stomp him with our feet," Desperado suggested while his eyes never left the cat.

"Let's ignore him so he doesn't know we know he's there. We should give him time to get closer. We need to keep the others quiet,"

Ali said. *"You keep an eye on him and I'll let the other horses know what we're doing. The kids are sleeping. I hope they stay that way for a little while."*

Ali turned nonchalantly and whispered to the other horses what he and Desperado planned to do. They all agreed to help. Very slowly the horses moved and got into position as they covertly watched the cat creeping along the wall of the canyon.

When the cat reached a spot about twenty feet from where the kids and Hilda lay sleeping, Ali nodded his head and Desperado screamed the stallion challenge. With Desperado leading, all ten horses rushed the cat at the same time. The cat didn't see that coming. His prey had never turned on him and certainly not in a group. He snarled and spit, turned and ran while the horses charged him from behind. He was halfway out of the canyon before Todd and Becky sat up to see what was happening. They watched as Desperado led the charge at something large and tawny streaking to the canyon opening. They heard the cat's snarls and knew what it was immediately. The others sat up too watching the horses running toward the mouth of the canyon. At first, they thought the horses were running away and began calling them back in panic.

The horses stopped in a bunch as soon as the cat streaked out of the canyon. They turned and walked nonchalantly back to the pond as if nothing happened. Todd found the paw prints only a few feet from where they were sleeping. The prints were huge. He pointed them out to the others.

"Looks like our horses saved us again," Todd told the group. "Those look like mountain lion prints and from the size of them, it was a big one. Did you notice Desperado leading the charge?"

Everyone had to look at the prints. They shivered when they realized how close that big cat came to them. Everyone including Hilda hugged the horses and praised them for their bravery. They shuddered as they thought about what could have happened. Hilda paid special attention to Annabella. She seemed a bit short of air for the exertion. She was in her late teens and hadn't had that much excitement for many years. Hilda worried about her but she soon calmed down and began grazing on the grass around the pond. In reality, she was almost as excited about her son's intelligence in stopping a potential slaughter than she was about the extreme exercise it brought her for a short period of time. Her breathing slowed back to normal not as quickly as the others, but for her age pretty quickly for the situation. She was intensely proud of her son.

Once things settled down in the canyon and the kids' heart rates returned to normal, they talked about it. Todd was so proud of Desperado; he could have popped the buttons off his shirt. "Did you see who was leading the pack after that ol' cougar?" he said.

Becky chimed in, "Yeah, I can't believe they chased that thing! Prince Ali was a half-step behind him and I know he's been attacked by one of those before."

"I always thought horses would run from a predator like that," Charlie said. "I've never heard of horses chasing one before."

Hilda remembered the young Desperado before she sent him to Chris O'Neal for training. He was a trickster. Desperado loved to sneak up behind her while she was bent over working in her kitchen garden. Sometimes he sneaked up and goosed her. Sometimes he'd overturn her wheelbarrow or try to drag her rake away. She smiled remembering what a character he was. She was proud of him. Desperado managed to get them to this canyon safely and he led the charge to keep the predator away from her and the kids. He was big and strong and powerful and she loved him dearly. With 40 years of breeding experience, she knew he was the finest horse she and Jan ever brought into this world. She wished Jan could be here with them now and see how Desperado turned out. Jan would be as proud of him as she was. It brought a tear to her eye.

Todd remembered Desperado when he came to Cold Water Creek Ranch as a lanky two-year-old. The grooms had to watch their ball caps or Desperado would snatch them and toss them across the barn. Pocket rags were fair game too. Within days of his arrival, Chris was called to the barn before he finished his first cup of coffee one morning. The feed crew discovered Desperado's stall door open and the horse missing. They searched the entire ranch. He was nowhere to be found. Chris was mighty upset when he called Jan Jorgenson to let him know they couldn't find Desperado.

Jan laughed when Chris explained the horse managed to open his stall door and disappear. "Did I forget to tell you about that?" Jan said. "That youngster is an escape artist for sure. I never did find a latch that could hold him in his stall if he wanted to go walkabout. I'll bet he's here or close by. I'll go look for him and bring him back."

Todd loved that young horse. He had a sense of humor. He loved everyone and he teased them all with his pranks. At the same time, he was a handsome Arabian horse in all the right ways. His bay coat gleamed. His white markings stood out against his brown body that was so dark it was nearly black. His movements were graceful and sparing as they should be in a Western horse.

Desperado spent a few months with Chris O'Neal and went back home until he was ready for saddle training. Todd missed the horse terribly while he was gone but felt elated when Hilda returned him for training after Jan passed away. He took to training like a duck to water. He loved working. Todd watched his dad work with Desperado as often as he could. He was itching to climb aboard himself and take a spin on him.

He talked to his dad over dinner one night. "Dad, do you think Desperado could be a youth horse?" he asked. Chris mulled the thought around and said, "Yes, I think he could. I think he might be great in the 13-and Under Western classes. I'll talk to Hilda about that. Maybe you'd like to take him to a show?"

That was the answer Todd was hoping for. "Oh, yes, Dad! I'd love to ride him. He's my favorite of all your training horses next to Prince Ali. Ali is Becky's horse. Maybe Hilda would let me be Desperado's rider."

Hilda was pleased to have a young rider with Todd's talent ride her horse. The two did very well together. Chris continued working with Desperado and turned him into an excellent Reining horse as well as a winning Western Pleasure horse. Desperado could do the sliding stops without a single hop and his spins were perfect, fast, and straight. His flying lead changes in the figure eight patterns were as good as they get. He and Todd were a team about as talented as they come. The strong connection between horse and rider was obvious to anyone that watched them.

CHAPTER NINE

As dawn broke through the darkness, the smoky smell of the fire permeated the air over the entire area. Exhausted and hungry men and women returned to the temporary fire camp at the ranch south of Cold Water Creek Ranch for rest and food. New crews dispatched to take their places at the head of the fire. Airplanes again lumbered into the sky with their loads of water and fire retardant. Helicopters refilled their belly buckets and turned toward the head of the fire which now stretched miles across. Ground crews went into the forest behind the fire to mop up hot spots where they could do so safely. Dozer engines choked and sputtered as they started back up and headed out to clear more trees and land in an attempt to stop the deadly northward march of the beast. Crews came in from neighboring states to lend their hands and backs to the effort. Wyoming was in a direct line. Their fire crews established wide firebreaks on their own territory in case the fire reached them. Additional air support flew in from other states to help drop water and fire retardant on the blaze. There were thousands of men and women dedicated to stopping this fire and willing to expend whatever effort was necessary to do so.

The Fire Chief sent up two helicopters for reconnaissance. He needed first-hand reports about the fire. The chopper pilots headed north above the heart of the fire and sent back their visual findings. The Chief used those reports to move assets around in the field to get ahead of the fire and stop it in its tracks.

One of the chopper pilots reported the sighting of the nine kids after his second pass over the canyon where they holed-up for the night. The canyon was surrounded on two sides by active fire. There was no way to get the kids and their horses out of there so the decision was made to drop supplies to them. Chief Odom personally found Chris O'Neal to let him know the kids were spotted in a safe area for the moment. He told him he was having supplies dropped in for them and what the general situation was. They could not get to the kids for a while, maybe the next day if they were lucky. The Chief had a satellite phone added to the supplies on the outside chance one of them could figure out how to use it properly. He didn't really expect them to.

Chief Odom was startled to get the call from Todd O'Neal a few hours after the supplies were dropped in the canyon by helicopters. He made it a point to find Chris again and let him know what Todd told him. Chris shared the news with the other parents at Cold Water Creek Ranch. As exhausted as they all were by that time, the knowledge that the kids and their horses were safe for the moment buoyed their spirits.

With all the extra animals at Cold Water Creek Ranch, the family members of the trapped kids pitched in and worked through the day. Chris's normal workers were unable to get to the ranch because of roadblocks on the highway. Some of the women kept up the coffee and ice tea service from Sharon's kitchen. A couple of them went to the camp south of the ranch which was providing rest and food for the firefighters. They pitched in there. They helped cook on the grills and served the men and women taking rest-breaks from the firefight. They had another very long and worrisome night.

The recon helicopter took off at first light the next morning to check on the fire's progress through the night and do a flyover of the canyon where the kids and horses were trapped. He reported back that the firebreaks and the fire retardant were making headway. The northward progress of the fire had been stopped in a few places. Ground crews handled spot fires there with engines and old-fashioned picks and shovels. They were beginning to win!

As he flew over the canyon he saw the neat row of tents and the kids waving. He checked the area east of the canyon and saw what he thought was a way into the canyon. It would take some time and heavy equipment, but he thought they might be able to get to the group within a day. He reported his findings to the Chief directly.

Chief Odom had another problem on his hands now. The Public Information Officer reported the missing kids to the media sometime during a briefing the day before. One enterprising reporter reached the Arabian Horse Association in Denver and got a list of the kids who'd been competing in Albuquerque, New Mexico the week before and spotted something newsworthy. He'd done more checking and found out which kids and horses were associated with Cold Water Creek Ranch at that competition. He zeroed in on two names – Prince Ali and Becky Howard. They'd been all over the news a few months ago when the 2.5 million dollar stallion was stolen from the Swallows Day Parade in San Juan Capistrano, California and the thieves left Becky in a coma.

The reporter was sitting on national news! If Prince Ali was one of the horses trapped by the fire, this would hit the newspapers and TV across the nation and possibly even beyond that. He had to get confirmation somehow. He wanted credit for this one. A news story of this size might get him out of the *Colorado Daily* in Boulder and into one of the big markets, like New York or Los Angeles.

Harvey Thurman tried every way he could think of to get past the roadblocks on the highway. He had to get to Cold Water Creek Ranch to confirm Prince Ali was among the missing. The Forest Service personnel were not cooperating. The Highway Patrol personnel were not cooperating. No one would let him through the roadblocks especially because the Command and Control vehicle and personnel were all at Cold Water Creek Ranch themselves. Chief Odom would have the badges of anyone who let a reporter through and they knew it.

The Chief got several calls about Harvey Thurman. He didn't have time to talk to the man. He had his hands full with thousands of men and women fighting the largest blaze in this area in recorded history. Hundreds of home and ranch owners depended on him and his strategies to save their homes and livelihoods. He didn't have time to waste on a single reporter.

Harvey Thurman was resourceful. He was an outdoorsman. He liked to hunt and fish. He hiked, skied and loved water sports. He also owned a four-wheel two-seat off-road machine. When all else failed him, he pulled that out, gassed it up, added a couple of extra five-gallon cans of gas on the back and headed out into the forest. If he couldn't use the highway, he'd find another way. The way was rough going. There were no roads, only animal trails to follow. He had to cross over several brooks and streams which dumped into Boulder Creek at some point. He knew approximately where he was going but hoped he'd recognize it when he saw it.

It took him almost five hours. He was behind the rear gate of Cold Water Creek Ranch when he recognized the Fire Service Command and Control Vehicle. He hid his four-wheeler in the woods and walked through the gate to the house looking for Chris O'Neal. One of the ladies directed him to the barn.

Harvey introduced himself to Chris. He asked him to confirm Prince Ali was among the missing horses and Becky Howard was among the missing kids. Walter Howard was in the barn and heard his daughter's name mentioned and joined the conversation. Harvey's heart rate zoomed. He had his scoop! Between Walter and Chris, he got the names of Charlie Reeves, another Boulder youth, Chris's son, Todd, and the one boy and five girls from California too. He had a breaking story to deliver. He asked Chris if he could use the barn office for a minute. He called the news editor at the *Colorado Daily* in Boulder and spilled everything he knew. He dictated the story by phone to the editor.

The news editor in Boulder broke the news and it hit the AP wire within minutes. The story was picked up by every news service in the country. Photos of Prince Ali and Becky Howard were pulled from the archives and made the front pages again as well as the late afternoon telecasts from the major TV stations across the nation. The Boulder fire was headline news everywhere with a 2.5 million dollar stallion in the mix. Harvey Thurman was jumping with excitement as he headed back to Boulder on his four-wheel vehicle.

Chief Odom had no idea Prince Ali and Becky Howard were part of the group of kids trapped by the fire until his supervisors called him. He and his wife knew the Howards and Prince Ali well. The Chief talked with his superiors about how he might rescue the kids and horses. He studied maps for the canyon the chopper pilot pinpointed by his onboard GPS.

The mouth of that canyon was several miles off the highway in undeveloped land. Getting to it would require bulldozing a road in for engines and ground crews. It would take hours to get there and would take back-breaking work every inch of the way. Chief Odom only had a few hours of daylight left. He decided to make a start on the job and see how much his crews could get done before they lost the light. The pressure was on him now since news about Prince Ali and Becky Howard being trapped in the canyon got out.

CHAPTER TEN

The Arson Investigation Team arrived at the mansion construction site as soon as they could safely do so. Fire crews poured enough water on the burning framing timbers to extinguish the fire the afternoon it started. The team consisted of three men, two experienced arson investigators and one who'd just finished his schooling and was in the field for the first time. The lead investigator was Buck Martin.

Buck had been around for 30 years with the fire department. He was something of a hero to the newer hires. He started as one of the fire crew and worked his way up. He got his education at night and became an arson investigator for the Boulder City Fire Department. He'd investigated a lot of suspicious fires; businesses on the brink of bankruptcy, homes going into foreclosure, cars about to be repossessed, homes of the hated ex-spouse or business partner, etc. People had lots of reasons to burn things up, mostly bad reasons. And there were lots of sloppy ways to start a fire. He saw the gas can used to burn a car left in the back seat. He found the melted Bic lighters. He walked into a burned out home and saw where someone had actually piled charcoal briquettes on the couch and used barbecue lighter fluid to start the fire right in the living room.

Most people believe the evidence will be burned up in the fire. They are often wrong. Buck could smell accelerant. He looked for burn patterns which told him where and how the fire was started. He told the younger guys, "The signs are all there. All you need to do is learn how to read them."

Buck walked over the concrete foundation looking at the burned studs shaking his head. This would have been a very large building had the fire not knocked it down. He didn't see any evidence the fire started in the mess here. He noted in the original reports one of the firemen thought they'd found the remains of incendiary devices on some trees across the brook. He found a narrow area along the stream and jumped across. When he looked at the south side of the cottonwood trees he found what he was looking for. The burn patterns on the trees were clear. He used his knife to pull what looked like a staple out of one tree where the bark was burned the heaviest. He was sure that was where a device was attached to the tree. He put it in an evidence bag he pulled from his pocket. He could see where flammable material dropped onto the leaf pile at the base of the tree and how the flames went up the bark on that side. A portion of the tree was burned but the fire never got hot enough to burn deep enough into the tree to kill it. Over time, new bark would form around the burn area to protect the internal structures of the tree. One of the four trees was burned more seriously than the others. That one might or might not survive. He dug around in the remainder of the leaf piles at the bases of the trees. He could see where the wind pushed the top layer of burning leaves and embers around the trees and across the brook. He figured that was the likely cause of the fire in the framing structure. He hopped back over the brook and followed the burn path there right up to the foundation of the structure. He also followed burn paths directly into shrubs and natural leaf piles at the bases of trees to the north and west of the foundation. He could see the conflagration in his mind.

Buck walked back to the brook and walked up and down the bank looking along the edges for anything out of the ordinary. He knew it when he spotted it. One of the devices had blown off a cottonwood tree and hit the water. The water extinguished the flames. The current pushed it downstream for a way until what remained of an incendiary device caught on rocks along the edge of the brook. He took photos and then used a stick to pick it up. Scorch marks on it proved him correct. He pulled a larger evidence bag out of his pocket and placed the device inside. He carefully marked the bag with the exact location where he found it.

He called the other two men over and showed them the south side of the trees, the staple, and the remains of the object he found in the brook. They all walked back to the driveway area of the mansion and gave that a hard look too. Clear as day there were tracks from tires that appeared to skid somewhat at the bottom of the driveway. "Looks like he took off in a hurry," Buck said. "Let's measure the tire marks and the width and see if that will tell us anything." Buck took photos just as he had taken photos of the trees and the mess left on the building foundation. The rookie saw the blood and pointed it out. "Good catch there, Steve. If this came from the perp, we might have DNA." Buck told him. Buck pulled out his test kit and poured some liquid on a large swab. He dragged the swab over one of the blood drops on the concrete. It turned pink/purple immediately. "This is definitely blood. Let's take more swabs and let the lab tell us if it's human or not. Since the drops are round, they appear to have fallen straight down from something not more than four feet high. Could be a person.

Maybe the idiot cut himself while he fixed up these crazy incendiary devices. Those things might have worked inside a building but certainly not out here on a tree." Buck couldn't imagine what he was thinking, but then again, he's an arsonist. Buck shook his head. He thought about all the carnage the man caused, all the dead animals, all the destroyed habitat, all the homes he knew had burned to the ground, and he'd even heard unsubstantiated rumors there had been several deaths in this fire. 'Idiot' was not a strong enough word to describe a person who would cause all this. It made Buck mad and sad at the same time. He vowed to help catch whoever it was so he would pay for what he'd done here.

There was no other evidence to gather. "I think we're done here," he said when he was satisfied. "Let's put the word out through the Public Information Officer that we are looking for any witness that saw a vehicle in this driveway or leaving it around the time of the fire."

Once Buck got back to his office and the lab, he turned the evidence over for evaluation. He began making phone calls. He called every contractor of record that worked on the construction site. None of them had personnel at the job site that day. One of them had some interesting things to say about the owner though. They made the hackles on the back of Buck's neck stand up. According to the contractor, he was the third General Contractor for that building and it was only in the framing stages. The first two were fired because they refused to do work against building codes without plan changes being approved by the county planning office.

The owner was difficult to work for and very demanding. He'd brought his wife to the building site once while the General Contractor was there. She wanted a bridge added over the brook and another deck built so she and her friends could sun themselves. Four cottonwood trees were in the way. The owner wanted them removed. The planning office refused to allow that. The cottonwood trees were over 200 years old and protected by law. Building a deck for some vain woman to enjoy was not a good reason to take them down. The owner was furious and threatened to fire everyone working on the job.

The following morning, the Public Information Officer called Buck. "We did get a couple of calls on that construction site. All of them saw a vehicle in the driveway before the fire broke out. They remarked it was a strange vehicle to be at a construction site and assumed it might have been the owner."

"Why was that?" Buck asked. "What kind of vehicle was it?"

"All of the witnesses said they saw a new Chevrolet Corvette in the driveway. The reason it jumped out at them was the color. It was bright red and hard to miss. One of them even gave me the license plate number. Are you ready for this? He said it was a Colorado plate that read": 'R E D H O T'. If that was the arsonist, it appears he likes to advertise."

Buck thanked him for the call and immediately called the Department of Motor Vehicles in Denver. He asked for information on a newer Chevy Corvette with the plate 'R E D H O T' and got a name and address in Denver.

Buck called the Fire Chief and gave him a full report on what he knew to date. He told Chief Odom he would be involving the Denver Police Department in the case and attempt to pick up the perp as soon as possible. Chief Odom told him he also had news that would affect the case. There were three deaths discovered as his people were doing their survey of the damage. Two older people died in their burned-out home. Apparently, the fire caught them off guard at the beginning and they couldn't get out before their home was overrun. The other death was in a car. A woman was trying to escape and died when the fire overcame her in her car. There were murder charges to pile on the person who set the fire.

CHAPTER ELEVEN

Once the big cat scare was behind them, the nine young people and Hilda found themselves cold and very hungry. They'd eaten everything they brought with them and there was not one thing edible in this rocky canyon. They did have water and the horses had some grass left around the edges of the pond to graze on. The horses were doing better than the humans.

Todd and Charlie walked to the opening of the canyon and looked around. Trees were still burning outside the canyon opening. The smoke was thick and the ash even thicker. They saw no one and heard nothing but falling limbs and trees as they burned. It wasn't safe to leave the canyon yet. They returned and told the others what they found.

Hilda did her best to keep their spirits up. "At least we have fresh water here. That will help us and the horses. We may be here for a while. I thought I heard airplanes overhead. Maybe we'll get lucky and one of them will fly over this place and spot us. You guys are young and healthy. You won't die if you miss a meal or two. We're safe if we stick together and stay right here. You know, I think those horses will protect us. Look how they took off after that cat. He ran screaming out of here like his tail was on fire!" she laughed.

Under the circumstances, Hilda's humor was catching. The kids all had a good laugh over the cat comment. The morning sun warmed the air so they no longer shivered from cold. There was nothing they could do about the empty feeling in their bellies. They watched the horses grazing on grass and were envious.

Suzie was quiet and didn't have much to say. She walked about halfway to the entrance of the canyon and pulled herself up on a large boulder. She sat staring at the entrance as tears rolled down her cheeks. No one noticed her for a while. Heidi finally looked around and spotted her and walked over. Heidi noticed the tears, climbed up on the boulder next to her and asked, "Hey, what's wrong with you?"

Suzie broke down completely and sobbed, "This is all my fault! If I hadn't decided to take off, we'd be back at the ranch right now."

Heidi put her arm around Suzie's shoulder and hugged her. "Hey, don't you take all this on you. Yeah, we were pretty stupid but you don't control a forest fire. You didn't start that."

"I know, but maybe we'd be back at the ranch if I hadn't insisted and taken off like that," Suzie sobbed. "I don't know if I can face the others. I know they're going to blame me for this."

"Nobody is blaming you," Heidi said. "Come on back. We're just going to hang out here until we can leave the canyon and ride back to the ranch.

"Give me a minute, will ya. I don't want to go back looking like I was crying," Suzie said.

"Just to change the subject, what did you think of the horses chasing that mountain lion this morning?" Heidi asked. "I've never heard of such a thing before. Gosh, that cat was huge and he sure was in a hurry to get out of here with ten horses on his tail, wasn't he?"

Suzie perked up. "Yeah! I couldn't believe my horse was in on that. Wow, that was something, wasn't it?"

Heidi and Suzie chatted on for a few more minutes about how brave their horses were which was exactly what Heidi had intended. Once she was sure her best friend was calm, she hopped off the boulder and joined the others near the pool.

When Heidi came and sat down in the circle made by the others, Becky asked her under her breath, "What's going on with Suzie?"

Heidi sighed and shook her head. "You don't know what it's like for her. I don't think anything she's ever done is good enough for her mother. If she works her fanny off and gets a 'B' grade in school, her mother tells her if she'd worked just a little harder she'd get an 'A'. I've heard it myself. I can't imagine why her mom is so critical of her. I don't know why she's so mean to her. I'm pretty sure that's why she acts out sometimes, like when she said dumb things in the barn about Maryann, and when she decided to take off yesterday. I think she's just rebelling and doesn't know how to do it right. She's really kind-hearted, smart and talented. Maybe she just needs to grow up some more."

"She came to me and apologized in private for that, you know," Maryann said. "And look at the team we were at the Nationals. Everyone, including Suzie, helped each other out every single day of the competition. I think we need to get that team spirit back again right now if we are going to get out of this mess. None of us blame her for the fire. We don't even know how that started. What we must do is stick together no matter whose dumb decision helped get us here."

None the boys had much to say but they and Hilda agreed with Maryann. They had to stick together no matter what.

Several hours later the sound of a helicopter thump-thump-thumped overhead and echoed through the canyon. The kids stood in a circle holding hands waiting for it to appear over the wall of the canyon so they could see it. The human circle was their idea to make themselves seen by the pilot if he did fly over them. When the helicopter came in sight over the ridgeline, the kids jumped up and down and waved and screamed for the pilot to notice them. The pilot was almost over the canyon before he noticed something moving on the bottom that didn't look right. The winds were blowing him around in the air and he passed over the opposite ridgeline before he was sure what he saw.

Word about the missing kids went out to everyone working the fire in any capacity the minute the Fire Chief confirmed the story. The ground crews hoped they didn't find the kids overrun by fire and dead somewhere in the woods. The pilots of the planes dropping water or fire retardant or doing recon were looking for signs of them from the air.

The kids saw the helicopter fly over the other side of the canyon and sat down in disappointment. Maryann and Susie looked like they were about to cry. They continued hearing the thump-thump-thump of the machine and it began to get louder again. Everyone stood up and watched the sky, holding their breaths. The helicopter flew back over the top of the canyon wall so the pilot could get a better look. He saw the horses grazing and thought they were a herd of elk at first until he realized there were several white animals in the group. Elk didn't come in that color! Then he saw the kids jumping up and down and knew he'd found the missing group. He dropped lower for a better look but had to climb again when he got caught in a downdraft. The air was treacherous and there was no room to land safely so he picked up his radio and called in a report. The pilot was on his way back to his base when he spotted the group in the canyon so after his second pass and the confirmation of what he saw, he continued back to base.

The group in the canyon began to get excited when the chopper made the second pass over the canyon. Maybe they'd been spotted. Maybe someone could help them. The chopper pilot had no way to communicate with them on the ground. When he had to pull up sharply and sped off the kids weren't sure they'd been seen at all. Most of them were dejected. Hilda tried to cheer them up. "Give it some time. Rome wasn't built in a day, you know," she told them. "There's a chance he saw us and will report it. Just wait. That's all we can do anyway."

The pilot debriefed with his boss. "We can't get in that canyon safely with a chopper," he told him. "The downdrafts are terrible and there's not much room to maneuver. What we could do is notify the ground crews in the area. We have the GPS coordinates for the place. My recon showed it will be a while before we can get anyone in there to get them but we could drop supplies to them."

The pilot's boss notified Chief Odom and told him what the pilot suggested. Chief Odom ordered emergency supplies and had them delivered to the chopper pads. They were going to drop tents, sleeping bags, flashlights, meals ready to eat, a medical kit in case one was needed, and bottled water. Also included were 2 bales of hay for the horses. They packed a satellite phone in the kit so the kids could call and let them know if there were any medical emergencies they needed help with. That should hold the group for another day or two if necessary. Everyone at the ranch was jubilant over the news. All they had to do was wait it out.

Several hours after the helicopter left the area of the canyon for the second time, the kids and Hilda heard the

DESPERADO – WONDER HORSE THREE

thump-thump-thumping of choppers again, this time two of them. They were jubilant too. They'd been spotted! Someone knew where they were! They might get out of this yet.

One chopper at a time lowered a crate on a line into the center of the canyon. The kids stepped back. The first crate was released and thudded to the ground. The chopper lifted and flew off to the south as the second chopper lowered another crate and dropped it next to the first one. That chopper also lifted and flew away south leaving the canyon quiet once again.

The kids attacked the crates and found the food right away. They were ready to sit right down and eat until Hilda cautioned them. "Let's see what they gave us before we eat. If we need to get something set up we should do that first. We are going to lose the light soon." The kids began tugging items out of the crates and lining them up in rows. Once they had everything out of the crates, they took fresh hay to the horses and began setting up the tents. It would be dark again within a couple of hours. At least tonight they would have shelter and warmth for the night and flashlights so they could see in the darkness. Todd, Brody, and Charlie took the satellite phone and looked at the instructions that came with it. They were a little afraid of it since it came with stickers on the phone and on the box that read, "Property of the U.S. Government." Brody was a near genius with electronic stuff. He studied the instructions as fast as he could. Charlie held the phone while Brody read the instructions out loud and told them what to do. Todd took Brody's instructions for the other equipment including the portable antennae. Charlie found the buttons referred to and pointed them out to Todd.

The only phone number they could reach with that satellite phone was the Fire Chief in charge. They followed instructions carefully and tried out the phone. Todd dialed the number given in the instructions. The call went directly to the Command and Control Center vehicle where Chief Odom was coordinating the firefighting efforts. The Chief picked up the phone.

"Chief Odom here," he said. "Who is this?"

Todd, a little shaken to reach the actual Fire Chief hesitated a second and said, "Um, Chief, Sir, this is Todd O'Neal. I'm with a group of friends who were riding horseback when the fire came up behind us."

"Young man, I'm certainly glad to hear from you!" the Chief answered. "Are you all together and are you all okay?"

"Yes, Sir, we are fine and thank you for the tents and stuff, especially the food. We were getting hungry," he said. "Can you let my dad know we're okay?"

"I'll call him the minute we get off the phone," the Chief told him. "Do you need anything else?"

"Sir, just one more thing," Todd said. "Can you tell my dad that Hilda Jorgensen is with us too? When the fire came up behind us we stopped by her ranch and got her. She's older and doesn't drive. My mom takes her shopping and to the doctors and stuff. The fire was about to overrun her place so we just put her up on a horse and took her with us. Do you know if her ranch was saved?"

"I'm sorry, Todd," Chief Odom told him. "We haven't done the survey of property damage yet. We are concentrating on setting fire lines and surrounding the fire. Our crews have been working to protect property as best they can but we have not had time to see what has been lost yet."

"I don't want to keep you, Sir," Todd told him. "I know you are very busy with stuff right now but will you also tell my Dad and Mom that I love them? The other kids here want their parents to know that too. We'll be fine. Nobody's been hurt. The horses are great. Hilda is in good shape too. And tell the helicopter pilots we appreciate them dropping supplies to us. Thank you."

The call disconnected. The boys carefully turned it off so the batteries wouldn't run down and put it back in the box with the instructions. It was a tool they might need again.

CHAPTER TWELVE

Another long, dark night faced those in the isolated canyon. They were almost out of hay for the horses but they still had enough food for themselves for dinner and breakfast in the morning. The tents and sleeping bags kept them warm and comfortable. Brody and Todd tried out the satellite phone one time late in the afternoon to let Chief Odom know they were all doing fine. Todd told him about his concern for Hilda because she'd not had her medications since the fire broke out. He was worried about her. The Chief talked to Sharon O'Neal about it. Todd had mentioned in his first call that Sharon took Hilda to her doctor appointments. The Chief suggested Sharon call Hilda's doctor and get medications ordered for her through him. He already knew Hilda Jorgenson's home was gone. For the moment he kept that news to himself.

The relatives of the trapped kids continued their support efforts, including Charles and Celeste Carnegie, Maryann's grandparents, who worked like Trojans despite their ages. The group at the ranch caught two and three-hour cat-naps when they fell from exhaustion and got up and kept on moving. It was better than worrying themselves crazy over their missing kids and horses. They knew the media was aware Prince Ali and Becky were trapped by the fire. By that time Walter and Caroline Howard were just one of the group of parents. The parents fussed a bit about the press attention this situation was getting. Every parent at Cold Water Creek Ranch wanted their youngster safe and they wanted privacy when they were reunited. Now they were afraid it would be a media-circus that involved all of the young people, not just Becky and Ali. News people found the official photographer for the Arabian Youth National Championship Show and got copies of photos taken during the event. Pictures of all of the kids were in the news now.

Back in his office in San Francisco, Henry Babcock was tuned in to the TV coverage of the Colorado fire. When he saw Prince Ali and Becky Howard, he recognized them from earlier broadcasts after Prince Ali was horse-napped from San Juan Capistrano. The next photo on the screen was Desperado with Todd O'Neal. Henry jerked to attention with the name in the broadcast and stared at the TV screen. Yes, it definitely was that horse! That was the horse that tried to run him over on the riding trail and the horse that kicked the crud out of his rental car too. He was elated! Maybe he didn't need to spend a ton of money to buy him and torture him after all. He may have already been burned to death in a fire started because of Henry Babcock! Sometimes things just work out right. Henry whistled under his breath as he took his elevator to the ground floor on his way home. That TV Broadcast put the bounce back in his step.

Chief Odom's dozers and hand crews attacked the route to the canyon. There were many large trees still smoldering that needed to be pushed over or cut down and removed from the roadway the dozers were plowing. Spot fires had to be extinguished by hand or with water from the trucks that followed the dozers in. They made slow progress, but it was progress.

Chief Odom got good news from the front line. Fire breaks were holding the fire back. Winds had slowed so they were not pushing the fire as hard as before. A cold front from the west coast was making its way across the Rockies. Humidity levels were rising and clouds formed. The weather forecasts showed the possibility of rain. His teams on the front lines had 35% containment and were hammering away at the head of the fire. Maybe, just maybe, they could keep the destruction level down to 65,000 to 70,000 acres. His personal hope was to keep it to less than 90,000 acres. It was a big destructive fire but it looked like they were going to prevent it from crossing state lines into Wyoming. He silently prayed the weather would continue in their favor.

In the canyon, Prince Ali walked over to where Desperado grazed on the little grass still surrounding the pond. *"Hey, just wanted to ask you something,"* he said. *"How was it you knew to charge that cat thing that was prowling in here the other morning?"*

Mighty Max heard part of the conversation and his ears perked up. He walked over nonchalantly to join in. *"Yeah, how did you know to do that?"* he asked.

"Really, I didn't know, but what choices did we have? If we left it alone it could have attacked one of us or one of the kids. I wouldn't let that happen if there was something I could do to prevent it." Desperado said.

Schultzy was close enough to hear and chimed in. *"That thing was big and scary. My first instinct was to run. I'm glad you suggested doing what we did. I wouldn't want anything to happen to Heidi. That thing was close enough to hurt our humans. They can't run the way we can."*

"I figured we were bigger than it was. I don't think it expected us to turn on it. It probably thought we'd run away. I thought if we did

what it didn't expect, maybe we could make it run away instead," Desperado told them. *"And, that's how it worked out. I will remember that the next time a stray dog thinks he can chase me!"*

Prince Ali snorted, *"Yeah, I've had that happen too. Now I know what to do. Thanks, Desperado. Next time one of those yappy things comes at me I'll turn around and show him my hooves. Bet he'll run crying for his mamma the way that cat thing did!"*

The horses all enjoyed Ali's comment and snorted and nickered their delight. They kept nibbling on the few blades of fresh grass around the pond edge and the hay Todd, Brody and Charlie set out for them.

The dozers and hand crews started back at their work on the "road" to the canyon at first light. The lead fireman kept checking his GPS to make sure they were going in the right direction. Several areas were clear of brush and trees naturally so the work went faster there. By late afternoon, they could see the high cliff of the mountain and knew they were close. The lead fireman walked along the wall and found the opening of the canyon. He walked right in. He saw the horses grazing around the pond and the row of tents set up. He hollered, "Anyone here?"

Heads popped out of the tents and kids scrambled to their feet. They ran toward the fireman standing at the entrance in his helmet and turnout coat holding an ax on his shoulder.

"You kids okay?" the fireman asked as soon as they were near enough to hear. He dropped his ax head to the ground holding the handle.

"Oh, yes! We're fine. We can't wait to get out of here," Todd said. "You are a sight for sore eyes, Sir. Thank you for coming for us. Is it safe for us to leave here now? How soon can we go home?"

Hilda, slower than the bunch of the 13 and 14-year olds she was with, walked up to the fireman and took his hand.

"Thank you for coming. We're so happy to see you. I'm Hilda Jorgensen. These kids saved my life and took me with them before the fire reached my place. Do you know if it still stands?"

"Ma'am, I'm sorry but I don't have that information. I was assigned to build a road to this canyon so we can get you out of here. The fire is actually more than 35% contained now and the front is miles north of here. We're in pretty good shape now. We made a road from here back to the highway, about five or six miles. We've cleared it so we can get emergency vehicles in here if we need to. How are the horses? Will they need to be trailered out or can they make it out on their own four feet?"

Todd spoke up, "The horses are in good shape. We brought one extra horse with us from the Jorgenson's place without a halter and lead rope. The others have their bridles and saddles. Thank you guys for dropping hay for them when you dropped stuff for us. I don't think the grass around the pond back there would have been enough for all ten of them. We can saddle up and ride out whenever you give us the word."

"Let me check in with the boss. I need to talk to the dozer drivers too and make sure all the trees we needed to bring down are out of the way. I'll get right back to you. Please stay here until I come back. We don't need one of those 40-foot trees falling on you now," the lead fireman told them. He swung his ax back on his shoulder, turned and walked back out of the canyon to find his radio and call in the report.

Todd and the kids scrambled back to their camp and began saddling the horses. When they were given the okay, they wanted to get out of here as fast as they could. They wanted to get back to the ranch and their parents.

CHAPTER THIRTEEN

Buck Martin called the Denver Police Department and asked for their detectives on arson cases. He was put on hold for quite a while. Buck drifted off in his own thoughts while he waited and was jerked to attention when someone came on the line and announced, "Padilla here, what's your pleasure?"

Buck introduced himself and told the officer on the line he was working on the Boulder fire arson investigation. That immediately caught the interest of the officer on the other end of the line. "You mean the big one just north of Boulder that has everyone so worried?"

"Yeah, that's the one. I'm the lead investigator and we're very sure it was an arson fire. We have a couple of eyewitnesses that saw a vehicle parked at ground zero and one of them had the plate number from the car. I've run it through the Motor Vehicle Department and it points to a resident of your fair city. I'd like your help on this one."

"Sure, how can I help?" Officer Padilla asked.

"We have a name and address for the car. It belongs to a Mr. David Nyland," Buck told him and gave him the address from the motor vehicle registry.

"Yeah, we're familiar with him alright," Officer Padilla said. "I've had him in interrogation several times for arsons in the past couple of years. We've never been able to pin one on him though. The man is cagey as the devil himself and he leaves nothing that can incriminate him behind. No fingerprints, no financial records, no evidence at the scene, no nothing. I'd love to pin one on him. I know he's doing it, just can't prove it in court."

"You're going to love this case then," Buck said. "I have an incendiary device and at least three eyewitnesses that saw his car in the driveway of the site at the time the fire started. We may have DNA from blood evidence too. That will take a few more days. We need to find him and arrest him. I think we have plenty for a conviction. And, worse yet, we have three dead as a direct result of the fire, so we want him for murder as well as arson."

"Oh, man. That's awful! How soon can you get here? I'll get my team together. Meet us in the Lobby of the main Police Department Headquarters downtown. We'll get you to your address and pick the guy up," Padilla said.

Buck and his team took off for Denver. Buck called his boss and updated him on the case as they drove. Buck pulled to the curb in front of the multi-story Police Department Headquarters in downtown Denver two hours later. He called Padilla from the car.

"Wait where you are," Padilla told him "I'm bringing a team with me. We'll meet you at the curb and we'll lead you over there. Nyland lives in a townhome complex. I'm bringing enough guys in plain clothes to watch all the exits so he doesn't get away. We have some uniforms with us to block the driveways. We can box him in there. I don't know if the guy is armed or not."

A few minutes later a caravan of marked and unmarked Denver Police Department vehicles with one Boulder Fire Department SUV drove into an area of upscale condominiums and townhomes. The marked vehicles blocked the exits of one of the nicer townhome complexes while the unmarked ones and the Boulder FD vehicle parked along the curb on the side of the complex. Men in suits got out of the unmarked vehicles. The three wearing uniforms from the Boulder Fire Department joined them at the entrance. Padilla knew which townhome belonged to Nyland so he held a quick conference at the entrance with the other Denver personnel and those from Boulder. Several of the plainclothes officers split off to watch corridors on either side of their target address. Padilla and Buck's team went to Nyland's front door and knocked.

There was no answer at the door, so Padilla knocked again more forcefully. A man stepped out of the neighboring unit across the corridor, surprised to see the men at Nyland's door.

"He's not home," the man said. "He and his girlfriend left a couple of days ago."

"Any idea where he went?" Padilla asked as he opened his wallet and showed the man his badge.

The man's eyebrows went up in surprise. "Oh, what did he do?" he asked.

"We just need to ask him a few questions," Padilla answered. "Do you have any idea where we can find him?"

"Well, he and his girlfriend were supposed to go to Boulder for the weekend but they came back here early the same day. He was in a hurry for some reason. They went inside and were only there for a few minutes before they came back out. He was pulling two large suitcases. I overhead them talking in the hallway. Sounded like they were going to her place for her things and heading to the airport. I think I heard him say something about the Bahamas. He was in a real sweat though."

"Do you know what kind of car he was driving?" Padilla asked him.

"Yeah," the man laughed. "He and his girlfriend were going to shove all that luggage in his brand-new Chevy Corvette. I don't know what he was thinking. You can't get much more than a lunch box in one of them if you have two people in the seats."

"Did you ever notice the plate on his car?" Padilla asked.

"Oh, yeah," the man laughed again. "Red Hot! Did you ever see the guy? He's about 6'2" or 6'3" and if he's lucky he tips the scale at 170 pounds. He's got this crazy, fuzzy hair that sticks out everywhere except for the bald patch. His nose looks more like a beak to me. He reminds me of a scarecrow. My wife gets a kick out of him driving around in that fancy sports car with 'Red Hot' on the license like he's some Hollywood director or something. We couldn't believe it when he showed up with that woman. She's beautiful. He'd make a good clown. What a mismatched pair if there ever was one."

"Any idea what he does for a living?" Buck asked.

"He lives pretty well considering he's home most of the time. I have no idea where he gets his money but these townhomes aren't exactly cheap, you know. And that car he drives cost a pretty penny too. He's a good neighbor, picks up packages for us and keeps them at his place until we get home. But I don't recall him ever saying what he does now that you mention it. Maybe he works from home?"

"Thanks for the information," Padilla said offering the man his business card. "If you see him or hear from him, would you give me a call?"

"Sure, no problem. You guys have a good day," the man said as he turned and walked toward the parking garage.

"Bahamas?" Padilla said to Buck. "I'll get a search warrant for the townhome. We'll go through it and let you know what we find. I'll also call the airport and see if we can confirm his travel. The District Attorney needs to get involved and see what the extradition policy with the Bahamian government is. I'll keep you posted."

The men walked back to their cars. Padilla called off the marked units and everyone left the area. Buck was disappointed and angry. He wanted to see Nyland in handcuffs. He wanted him to see the destruction he caused. He wanted him to see the faces of the families of the people who died in that fire. He wanted him to pay for what he did.

CHAPTER FOURTEEN

The fireman hurried back to his truck and picked up the radio. He called Fire Chief Odom first. "Chief, we made it to the canyon where the kids and horses are. I've talked to them. They all appear to be in good shape; just a little scared is all. They told me the horses are all in good shape and they are anxious to get home. I also talked to Hilda Jorgensen, the older woman with them. She looks tired but otherwise okay. Our road is just about complete, only a quarter to half a mile or so from the mouth of the canyon. Those kids are really lucky. There is a straight wall of rock that protected the canyon. It has to be over a hundred feet high. The entrance is narrow, just about wide enough for a horse and rider to pass through. If we didn't have GPS coordinates, I don't know that we'd have found it at all."

"That's some of the best news I've heard all day," the Chief told him. "What are the conditions for getting them out right now?"

"Sir, the road is primitive at best. We might be able to get in with an ambulance, but it doesn't look like we need one at this point. We still have downed trees smoldering but the dozers have pushed over any that look likely to fall on the road they plowed in. It's rocky and uneven and hard to drive over in our trucks. The horses may have an easier time than we do with the vehicles. I'm concerned about getting them back to a safe zone though. There's no place along the side of the highway for them to travel on. We have many trucks out on that road. There are also property owners driving in to see what's left of their homes and ranches. I don't think it would be safe for them to use the highway."

"Got any idea how long it will take them to reach the highway?" Chief Odom asked.

"My guess is it will take several hours. The road isn't smooth. There are divots and holes all over it plus the rocks the dozers pulled to the surface. I'm not sure we can get them to the highway before nightfall. Maybe we should leave them where they are until first light in the morning. I can get supplies in for them with our four-wheel drive trucks."

"I'm concerned about the older woman. She's in her 80's. Should we try to get her out in one of our vehicles and get the kids out in the morning?" Chief Odom suggested.

"That's your call, Sir," the fireman said. "If we can get supplies in there, it might be better to leave her there with the kids. If they were mine, I'd feel better having someone there to keep an eye on them."

Chief Odom shook his head. He didn't know what he'd do if one of his kids were in that group. He decided to talk with Chris and some of the parents before making a decision. He turned over command to his Deputy Chief and went looking for Chris O'Neal.

He found Chris and Sharon and several of the other parents and gave them an update. The firemen in the field didn't think they could get the kids and horses out to the highway before dark. It was going to take several hours of hard travel to get there. The firemen felt it might be better to leave them in the canyon one more night and get them out at first light when they could see better. He told them what the fireman who actually saw and talked with the kids and Hilda said and what he saw for himself.

Chris and the other parents had lots of questions for the Fire Chief. He answered them all to the best of his knowledge. He made a decision.

"Here's the deal," Chief Odom said. "I think it best we leave the kids and horses in the canyon tonight. I can have four-wheel drive vehicles bring supplies and take one parent into the canyon. We can bring Hilda Jorgensen out and we can leave that parent with them for the night. That parent may have to walk out. Tomorrow when they reach the highway I will coordinate with the Highway Patrol to have the road blocked temporarily. We need several horse trailers at the exit point to load the horses to haul them back here. And there are actually 10 horses there. One of them came from the Jorgensen place without a halter or lead rope. The kids can ride back with the trailers or the Highway Patrol. I need you to select one parent, preferably one of you fathers, to go tonight. Chris, I need you to coordinate the trailers in the morning when they reach the highway."

Charles Carnegie was the first to volunteer. "I'll go. I'll stay with the kids. I think I can walk out of there."

Chief Odom looked at Grandpa Carnegie. "I think it would be better if one of the younger fathers went. I appreciate your offer, but we don't need another rescue on top of this rescue. According to my men, the walk out of there will not be a walk in the park. No offense meant but it might be a better job for a younger man. The kids are sleeping on rocky ground in sleeping bags inside small tents. The temperature drops pretty low at night. Todd told the fireman something about a mountain lion creeping around that got within 20 feet or so of the kids so I'd prefer one of the fathers that can take a rifle with him in just in case."

The mention of a mountain lion scared everyone. Charlie Reeves' dad stepped up. "Chief Odom I can handle a gun. I've been on elk hunts every year since I could remember. I've slept outdoors. I know all about cold nights and rocky ground. I'd like to volunteer to stay with the kids tonight."

Chief Odom looked at George Reeves and made a decision. George was in his late 30's and fit. He had a no-nonsense look about him. Don Odom decided he would be the perfect candidate. He was a local in the area. He was physically in good shape. He knew his way around a hunting rifle. He looked like he could make the five-mile walk if need be.

Chief Odom set up two four-wheel drive vehicles to haul hay for the horses and supplies for the kids. George Reeves dashed home for his hunting rifle and ammunition and made it back to Cold Water Creek Ranch to meet the fire vehicles for the drive in.

The drive to the canyon took nearly two hours covering a little over five miles. The vehicles bounced and jounced over rocks, roots and through holes and dips. They stopped at the rock wall before they lost the light for the day. George Reeves packed his rifle over his shoulder and picked up his ammo can in one hand and a package of meals-ready-to-eat in the other. He and the two drivers walked into the canyon together. They met a somber-looking group of kids. They had high hopes of riding their horses out that afternoon and were very disappointed when the Fire Chief decided they needed to stay one more night where they were. Charlie was overjoyed to see his dad! Todd, Brody, Charlie, George and the firemen hauled hay from the trucks inside to feed the horses and they brought extra supplies for the kids who were starving by that time.

It was fully dark before the firemen got on their way back to the highway with Hilda Jorgensen in the lead truck. They lit their overhead lights on the vehicles so they could see and follow their own vehicle tracks to avoid the other hazards on the make-shift road.

George helped the kids gather firewood in the waning light so they could build a fire inside the canyon for a bit of warmth. The horses were fed before the kids opened their own meals and settled down for what they hoped would be their last night in the canyon.

CHAPTER FIFTEEN

With George Reeves in the canyon with the kids, the parents felt more in control. One of them was with their kids. They all felt a little relieved. Hilda Jorgensen was delivered to Cold Water Creek Ranch by the firemen that night. The parents had a million questions for her about their kids. They wanted to hear about the mountain lion. Hilda assured them the kids were great. They were a nice bunch of young people and they were doing their best under difficult circumstances. Hilda told them how the horses chased the mountain lion from the canyon. Everyone was shocked. No one ever heard of a horse taking on a large predator like that. Horses were fight or flight animals. Horses would naturally choose flight when it came to a large carnivore attack.

Ginny Hartley spoke up, "I've worked with most of these youngsters. You have no idea how strong the bond really is between those horses and those kids. I could almost see that happening."

They were all thankful for George Reeves and his rifle when Hilda told them how close the cat got to where they were sleeping. She showed them with her two hands how large the paw prints of that cat were.

Hilda was glad to get out of the canyon but felt guilty leaving the youngsters there for another night. She'd had time to talk with all of them and she liked each of them personally. They were growing up and becoming wonderful young adults in her opinion. She had time to spend with each youngster and their horse while they were trapped together. There wasn't a horse in the group she wouldn't have welcomed into her own barn. Each horse had a personality that showed during the time in the canyon.

Desperado and Prince Ali exchanged leadership of the herd depending on the situation. Desperado was the one who led the group into the canyon in the first place and he was the one who led the charge on the mountain lion. He was more than Jan and Hilda expected when they bred his mother. He was a correct Arabian horse in every aspect, but he had even more attributes. He was smart. He was a good leader. He was dependable and looked after the others in the herd and the kids. He'd always had a sense of humor. Between Desperado and Prince Ali, Hilda felt safe in the canyon like her two big brothers were there to protect her.

Melissa's Mighty Max was a clown. He was always doing things that made Melissa and the others laugh. Maryann's La Duquesa was a queen. Everything she did, she did with elegance and dignity although she was a force to be reckoned with when she joined the herd chasing that mountain lion from the canyon. Heidi's Schultzy was like the bratty little kid who did things to annoy others but became contrite when called out on his shenanigans. He had a good heart and loved his Heidi like no other. Charlie's Aces High was a good ol' boy who wanted to please. Suzie's horse Chips was a lot like Aces High and very attached to Suzie. Kathy's Desi was somewhere between La Duquesa and Schultzy. He helped Schultzy pester the others but moved away with a certain dignity when called out for it. He obviously loved Kathy and hated to be on her bad side.

While Hilda was in the canyon her major problem had to do with sleeping on the rocky ground and cold temperatures at night. That was most uncomfortable for her old bones. She arrived at Cold Water Creek Ranch tired and achy all over and glad to be back in civilization. Chief Odom came to check in on her. She hesitated but finally asked him about her own home.

Chief Odom took her hand in his and looked right into her eyes. "I hate to be the bearer of bad news but according to my people, your home did not survive. They tried but could not save it."

With tears forming in her own eyes she looked at Chief Odom and said, "I know they did their best. If my home is gone, it is only wood and brick. The important parts of my life are in here," she tapped her finger over her heart. "Nothing can take that away from me as long as I am breathing."

Chief Odom gave her a hug before excusing himself. He had work to do and had to get back to it. When he stepped into the Command and Control vehicle, Buck Martin was on the phone for him.

"Buck, did you get him?" the Fire Chief asked.

"No. We didn't. We talked to one of his neighbors. He took his girlfriend to Boulder for the weekend and they came back to Denver early. The neighbor said he packed bags and said something about leaving for the Bahamas. Denver PD is working on it now. I've checked with the airlines and found he and a companion took a flight out the night the fire started. They had a flight to Miami connecting to the Bahamas. The Denver District Attorney is working with the Feds right now on extradition. We'll get him," Buck said. He grimaced over the last three words.

"This fire isn't out yet so I can't give an accurate cost of the damages yet but it will be substantial. We've not completed our survey of property damage yet. I know we've lost at least seven homes, many outbuildings, ten other homes were damaged, and there is dead livestock besides the damage to the forest itself. So far we've found the three people killed but there could be more. That guy has to pay for this."

"I couldn't agree with you more," Buck said. "I'm very sure we can nail him with this fire. Our lab found partial fingerprints on the incendiary device I scooped out of the brook. They were a match to the set the Denver Police Department has on file for him. He's been picked up on suspicion for arson before but never convicted. When we get this creep, we will squeeze him until he tells us who hired him. I have a strong suspicion we already know but his testimony will seal the deal. I think the property owner set this all up. All because his wife wanted a bridge over the brook that required four old cottonwood trees cut down. The county wouldn't approve that. Those trees are protected. They are over 200 years old for heaven's sake. They are burned but most of them will survive this. Too bad so many other things didn't including people."

"Have the Denver P.D. Detectives considered the owner's background yet? Would he be the kind of person that would do such a thing?" Chief Odom wanted to know.

"I'm not part of that investigation, Sir, but I will check with Officer Padilla and see. I did talk to the general contractor on the job. They were just finishing the framing stages and he was the third general contractor hired for the job. The county planning group was giving him a bad time about some of the things he wanted for the structure. Every time he wanted a change made, it had to go through the approval process again and there were changes that had to be made in other areas. It was dragging the job out and he was impatient as the devil. He also went through three other plumbers because he didn't like something they said or tried to explain to him. The General Contractor I talked to told me the guy has a very short fuse. He wants what he wants and he doesn't take 'No' for an answer well. The only thing he doesn't seem to care about is the money. If a change is going to cost him another couple of thousand dollars to move a door seven inches, he doesn't care; he just wants that door moved."

"I think you could be right about this. If the planners refused permission to chop down four trees he wanted to chop down, maybe he was nuts enough to try and have them burned down. Let's hope we can prove that. We have many homes lost and three people dead over four trees and his attitude of entitlement," Chief Odom said.

CHAPTER SIXTEEN

When the kids tacked up the horses in the canyon Desperado was relieved. He thought they would all be home that night. Unfortunately, the fireman came back into the canyon and told the group they wouldn't be leaving until morning. All the tack was removed and the horses left to graze on the little grass around the pond. Desperado had time to think about things.

Desperado loved Hilda and would do anything he could to protect her. He had loved Jan dearly too and still missed teasing him. He had some understanding about death and how final it was but couldn't conceive of that for himself.

Desperado and Todd made a perfect set. Todd could read Desperado like a book the same way Desperado could read Todd. He knew when Desperado was up to something. He knew when Desperado was off and when he was on. As a team, they won championships together. Todd could feel Desperado through the saddle and could turn him with the slightest touch on the reins or with a heel. Desperado loved the limelight of the winner's circle as much as Prince Ali did and he loved sharing that with Todd. He knew Hilda was officially his owner, but Todd was his 'heart-person' and always would be. He hoped one day it could become official. He'd seen other horses bought and sold. He didn't want to be one of those that just disappeared. He heard through the barn grapevine when one left to go to another state and the horses at Cold Water Creek Ranch never saw him again. He didn't want to think about being sold to Mr. Babcock. That scared him. Not seeing Todd would break his heart. But, this was now and that was in the future. He decided not to worry about it just yet. They still had to get back home.

Charlie was so happy to see his dad that night. When he came strolling through the entrance to the canyon with his rifle over his shoulder Charlie ran for him and almost threw himself into his arms and hugged him. He refused to cry even though he felt like it. George didn't mind one bit. He was glad to see his son and the other kids. George and Todd walked Hilda out of the canyon with the firemen so she could return to Cold Water Creek Ranch. Todd worried about her and was happy to see if only one of them got out that night, it was her. She was the closest thing he had to a grandmother. Through this ordeal, Todd was growing very fond of her. The rest of them could ride out when the sun came up in the morning.

In the waning light, Charlie, Todd, Brody, and George searched the area outside the mouth of the canyon for firewood and stacked what they found beside the tents. The girls broke open the bale of hay for the horses and scattered the flakes around near the pond. The boys built a circle of rocks to contain the fire pit and George lit the fire. For the first time since they became trapped, the kids had a warm fire that night. They had meals-ready-to-eat for dinner and talked with George about the past few days before turning in for the night. They had a busy day in the morning. They were going to leave the canyon at last.

Hilda faded fast. She was exhausted by the experience of racing ahead of the fire and nights in the canyon. Sharon O'Neal reached her doctor as Chief Odom suggested and renewed her prescriptions. She made sure Hilda had a decent meal and then walked her down the hallway to the entrance of the in-laws private quarters. She and Chris built that on their house years ago for Chris's parents. The in-law's area had a nice sized bedroom with private attached bathroom, a sitting room for reading or watching TV and a small kitchen with a table for four. There was a private outside entrance as well.

"Hilda, we're going to put you up in here for right now. You need a shower and a bed. I've put out fresh towels and clean nightclothes for you. Your medications are on the counter in the bathroom. If you need anything, please let me know. Thank you so much for watching over Todd and the others," Sharon said, hugging Hilda.

"I can just go to a hotel," Hilda protested. "I don't want to put anyone out."

"Not on your life!" Sharon scolded. "You can stay right here. You are almost part of the family, you know."

Hilda had a long, hot shower and tumbled into bed, asleep the minute her head hit the pillow. She dreamed about the mountain lion and watched as her pride and joy, Desperado, chased that thing out of the canyon snarling and spitting. Desperado's shoes struck sparks off rocks along the way and the canyon echoed his screams at the cat.

Officer Padilla put in extra time at his desk in Denver. He had another conversation with Buck Martin about the arsonist and the fire outside of Boulder. He was curious. He had several other cases on his caseload that he worked on during the day. This evening he wanted to see what he could find on the construction site owner after what Buck had told him. He started digging on his computer.

Henry Babcock started life as Vladimir Babachek in a New York City slum. He was smart and got good grades and worked part-time jobs to support his mother. His father was a drinker and died when his son was young. The report said he stepped off a curb into the path of a cab while intoxicated. Vladimir got his first real job at a brokerage on Wall Street. He supported his aging mother until her death when he was 25. That's when he changed his name to Henry Babcock. He was like a Donald Trump figure. He made money through the brokerage and started buying real estate. By the time he bought the property outside of Boulder, he was among the top five richest men in America. And he'd done that quietly. He didn't have the splashy personality of a Trump or Gates or any of the other very rich men. He didn't offer investment advice. He simply made money by the boatload. He didn't begin spending money until he married Savannah, his young and beautiful wife. He never socialized before meeting her either. What few photos Padilla could find showed a slightly older than middle-aged man with a balding pate and paunchy mid-section. He was so nondescript he would never be recognized in a crowd. Even the fact his suits probably cost close to $10K each would miss attention because they didn't look like anything special at all. He apparently had no flair for dressing or he did it intentionally.

There wasn't much written about him as a businessman either. There were a few innuendos about him not taking 'No' for an answer if he wanted something and a few people who refused to do business with him but wouldn't say why. The guy was almost like a ghost. Padilla was getting frustrated. The only legal issues he could find on the man were a slew of lawsuits against him or his companies over the years that were all suddenly dropped by the suing party. Nothing ever came to court. That raised a bunch of red flags for Padilla. Business suits were commonly settled but even that went through a judge. What was this guy's game anyway? He is almost never mentioned in the press, he makes money hand over fist, he buys whatever he wants, and he has few enemies that will talk about him. But he threw an old-fashioned hissy-fit on the construction site three times and fired contractors. What in the devil were they dealing with?

CHAPTER SEVENTEEN

Henry Babcock was mad as the devil. His brand new three-story ski chalet was destroyed. Everything that had been done would have to be done again right down to the foundation. Those four trees were still standing. His arsonist screwed up the job on an unbelievable scale. He'd started a darned forest fire trying to burn down four trees. There were reports of fatalities from the fire and many homes burned or destroyed as well. Nine kids and one old woman were missing. And his arsonist was missing too. He wasn't picking up the phone. He wasn't answering messages. He called his best man for this job, his "Special Projects Manager." The arsonist had to be found and Babcock wanted assurance he would never be able to tell anyone ever about his arrangements with him. The only bright spot in all of this was that horse, Desperado, was among the missing and feared dead in the fire.

When the tall in-descript man showed up in Babcock's office, Henry told him what he needed and handed him a large manila envelope. It contained a physical description of the arsonist with a photo and address with three large stacks of bills banded together. "I'll give you the balance when the job is done," was all Henry had to say before escorting the man to his private elevator. The tall man left Babcock's headquarters building in San Francisco and went directly to the airport.

The kids woke up at first light and spread the remaining hay out for the horses before having another meals-ready-to-eat breakfast with George Reeves. They took down the tents and rolled the sleeping bags up, piling them all near the entrance to the canyon. George made sure the fire pit from the night before was completely out and scattered. Then they waited. The firemen told George they would send in another four-wheel drive truck in the morning to pick up the tents and supplies so the kids could ride out unencumbered. George had his choice of riding out with the fireman or riding Annabella out with the kids.

The firemen arrived at the canyon a few minutes after the kids finished getting their horses ready to ride. The boys and George stowed the gear in the truck, including George's rifle and ammunition. He decided to walk out next to his son. He'd had the foresight to bring a halter and lead rope for Annabella so he would ride her or lead her along the pathway. The firemen turned the truck around and told them they would meet them at the road if they fell behind. The long march began. The road was rough. It was filled with rocks and stumps turned up by the dozers. There were holes and divots everywhere that could be ankle breakers if they weren't very careful. Even a couple of days past when the fire was active in this area, there were still trees smoldering and the kids heard several of them fall to the ground when their trunks would no longer hold them upright. It made a lot of racket in the forest and stirred up ashes and embers. It also spooked a few of the horses. Travel was slow, barely at a walk most of the way. It took several hours to traverse the road of a little more than six miles left by the dozers. At the end, they had to cross a ditch to reach the road. They stopped along the forest side of the ditch. If the four-wheel drive vehicles could get through that, they could on horseback.

The firemen they followed out met them across from the ditch and asked them to wait there while they called in their location to the Fire Chief. As soon as Chief Odom got word the kids were ready by the highway, he called the Highway Patrol so they could run a traffic break on the highway as soon as the horse trailers arrived. The Highway Patrol vehicles were the next to arrive. Chris O'Neal and three of the other parents had their trailers ready for the nod by Chief Odom. Chris lead the group north along the highway until they saw the Highway Patrol vehicles. They pulled to the side edge of the highway and waited until the Patrol officers blocked the road in both directions so the trailers could turn around and load the horses.

Everything went quickly and efficiently. Chris and the other parents opened the trailers and encouraged the kids across the ditch. Each horse was loaded and tied inside a trailer as quickly as possible. When all ten horses were inside and secure, the trailer doors were closed and drivers jumped back into the trucks ready to haul to Cold Water Creek Ranch. The kids and George Reeves also hopped into trucks and two of the Highway Patrol cars for the drive home. As soon as everyone was in and ready, the Highway Patrol let the trucks pull out onto the highway and they ended the blockade behind them.

The drive to Cold Water Creek Ranch was a short one. Todd O'Neal sat next to his father and Becky Howard sat next to Todd. There wasn't a word said during the drive home. Todd and Becky felt guilty for not doing what they were told on Monday morning before the trail ride set out. They knew they were in trouble with their parents and probably the other kids' parents as well. By not doing as they were asked, they had endangered their own lives and the lives of the other kids and the horses too. Becky sat in the truck with tears brimming in her eyes. Todd just sat there waiting to face the music he knew was coming.

The trailers were swarmed by parents and grandparents the minute they turned in the driveway. The horses were unloaded quickly at the barn and all were put in cross-ties so they could be untacked and brushed down. Everyone talked at once. Parents hugged their children and cried and laughed. Fire Chief Odom stopped in to check on them and welcome them home. The kids pulled the tack off their horses and brushed them down, checked their hooves and put them in bedded stalls as quickly as they could. Each horse got an extra ration of grain with their hay before the barn cleared out. Everyone moved into the O'Neal's living room. The canyon survivors were offered fresh sandwiches and milk or hot cocoa. Once the din settled down, Chris O'Neal asked the question that had been on the minds of the parents for several days.

"Just exactly what happened out there? When the fire broke out, I rode out to the meadow where you guys were supposed to be and found you gone. I followed your tracks until I couldn't go further because of the fire. We were worried sick about you," Chris said.

All nine of the young people started speaking at once. No one in the room could make hide nor hair of the conversation. Finally, Chris raised his voice and said, "One at a time please!"

Suzie stood up. "Let me take this," she said. Everyone in the room turned their eyes to her. "This was my fault. We had a great time in the meadow and we splashed in the brook. Then we had lunch and laid in the grass watching the clouds. But we hadn't seen any of the wild creatures, so I suggested we ride a little further. Todd tried to stop me, but I wouldn't listen. The others tried to talk me out of it, but I got mad and turned my horse up the trail and took off. Heidi's my best friend so she followed me. If anyone is to blame for this, it's me."

The room was completely silent for a minute while Suzie's confession sunk in. Suzie sat down on the couch and stared at her boots.

"The rest of us talked about it," Brody said. "We all heard what you said in the barn. But we watched Suzie and Heidi get farther and farther away. We decided you would be madder if we came back to the ranch and left them out in the woods by themselves. They could have gotten hurt out there alone. We decided not to leave them, so we hurried to catch up with them hoping to bring them back to the ranch before anyone found out about it."

"Dad," Todd said, "It's just like Brody said. The girls had no idea the danger they might be in out in the forest alone. We couldn't leave them. We didn't know what kind of danger we were all in until the smoke from the fire got so bad we could hardly see."

One by one, each of the young people spoke up and agreed with the comments made by Suzie, Brody, and Todd. Becky finally said, "If it weren't for the fire, we could have caught up to Suzie and Heidi and got back to the ranch with no one being the wiser. The fire was one of the dangers none of us thought about. Any or all of us could have burned to death out there if it hadn't been for Desperado."

"Really?" asked Chris. "Tell us about it."

"Todd was riding him so maybe he'd better fill you in," Becky answered.

"When I first smelled smoke, I thought it was someone having a barbecue. But the smoke kept getting worse and worse and we started hearing the fire behind us. That's when I knew we were in trouble. I didn't know what to do. Desperado took us to Hilda's home. By that time, we could see the fire behind us. I got Hilda up in Desperado's saddle and I climbed on the back. Hilda asked us to let Desperado's mother out of her stall so she didn't burn to death in there. Annabella stayed right with us. Desperado took us north, then west to the canyon where we would be safe from the fire, Dad. I don't know how he knew about it because we couldn't see the opening until we were right on top of it. There wasn't anything to eat in there but a small patch of grass around the pond. But the air was good and the water was clear and clean. At least we had that."

Kathy took her turn. "Yeah, you shoulda seen Desperado the next morning. There was a huge mountain lion that crept into the canyon while we were sleeping. Desperado screamed and charged the cat when he was only maybe twenty feet from us. All the other horses followed his lead and they chased that cat right out of the canyon. They saved our lives!"

Parents in the room hugged their kids and shuddered over the revelation. "We heard something about that from the firemen," Sharon O'Neal said quietly. "What a thing to witness!"

"Oh, there was a lot more," Melissa said. "When we were running from the fire, you should have seen all the wild critters that were also running away. Wasn't that bear and her cubs almost under Desperado's hooves at one point?" she asked Todd.

"Yeah," Todd answered. "You should have seen that ten-point buck we watched run smack into a tree. He fell down, then picked up his head and shook it, stood back up and ran off. That was funny and not funny at the same time."

Brody asked, "How about that mountain lion mother with her two kittens? They were good sized too but as scared as we were. They were making tracks to get out of there like they didn't even notice us at all."

One by one each of the youngsters told about their experiences in the canyon. They told about making a human circle and jumping up and down to attract the helicopter that spotted them and dropped supplies to them. They told how Brody, Charlie, and Todd took the satellite phone and learned how to work it so they could communicate they were okay. They thought Brody was a genius to figure that thing out. They told how the kids had scraped the ground with their bare hands to clear rocks so Hilda had a smoother place to sleep. They told how they took turns sleeping and watching in the dark so no other mountain lion would get so close to them again. They told how each of them helped others keep their spirits up so they didn't get discouraged about being trapped so far away from home and their families.

The more they talked about their situation, the more the parents realized how mature they'd acted under terrible conditions. Each of them made a contribution to the safety and comfort of others. They'd shared a couple of packages of crackers and bags of chips equally so they didn't go completely hungry the first night. They'd found a way to overcome most obstacles placed in their path. Even the walk out was shared equally. The lead horse and rider changed often to give them a rest and let them follow while someone else led for a while. They all admitted how happy they were to see George Reeves and his hunting rifle that last night. That was the first time they really felt safe since they left Cold Water Creek Ranch on Monday morning.

Todd suddenly looked around and didn't see who he was looking for. "Where's Hilda?" he asked.

Hilda slept a long time in a beautiful bed after her hot shower the night before. Her body ached from the cold nights and hard ground. She didn't wake up until late the next morning and fixed herself a cup of hot tea trying to decide if she should come out of the room in the bathrobe Sharon loaned her or not. Her clothes were a mess and she didn't have anything else to put on. Before she made up her mind, she heard a knock on the door. She answered it and Todd O'Neal threw his arms around her and hugged her. "How'd you sleep?" he asked her.

"I slept just fine as frog hair," she answered him with a twinkle in her eye. "Glad to see you home too. How's that rascal, Desperado?"

"He's great. He's out in his stall getting a bucket of corn and oats right now," Todd told her. "He looks like he didn't miss any meals. Speaking of which, why don't you come out and have something to eat yourself? Those meals-ready-to-eat didn't have much taste. My mom's cooking is better. Did you get your pills? Mom told me she talked to your doctor and got them for you."

"I thank you for thinking of me. I did get them and already took my morning ones with a cup of tea. You are sweet to think of that for me," she said and hugged him again.

"Well you are about as close as I get to a grandmother, you know," Todd told her. "I wouldn't want anything to happen to you."

"And you are a grandson anyone would be proud of," Hilda smiled.

CHAPTER EIGHTEEN

Officer Padilla hung up the phone and smiled. "Hey Arias!" he yelled at his partner in the next cubicle. "Just got off the phone with the District Attorney's office. We do have an extradition treaty with the Bahamas – especially if the person we want to get back here is wanted for Major Crimes against Humanity. Our Mr. Nyland certainly fits the profile. We want him for Arson, Destruction of Property, and Murder. They are contacting the Justice Department to see how we proceed. Do you know if Buck Martin got the DNA back from the blood he found in the driveway?"

"Let me check," Arias replied as he picked up the phone and dialed the number in Boulder.

Buck Martin was in his office and answered right away. He was just looking at his computer screen for the test results on the blood evidence he'd taken to the lab the day after the fire started. Officer Arias introduced himself as Officer Padilla's partner and asked if he had the blood results yet.

"Yeah, I was just looking that up. Let me see here…Yes! We have it. Seems we can now prove our Mr. Nyland was in the driveway of that home under construction. You guys must have collected from him before."

"I'm sure Padilla told you. We've picked him up several times for arsons here in the city. We did manage to get his DNA during one of his visits from a soda can. We've just never been able to find any blood evidence or DNA at any of the crime scenes before. That guy is slippery as an eel."

"I wouldn't give him points for brilliance though," Buck told him. "The incendiary device he was trying to burn trees down with would have worked fine inside a building, a warehouse, a home, or an office but NOT for something out of doors. The wind blew one of them clean off the tree and into the brook. I found that one myself. Now we know what he used before. I'm guessing he used some kind of tape to attach it inside but he had to staple it to the bark of the trees and left us the staples. The device would have burned completely in a closed environment so there would be nothing left to find except burn patterns and such. You'd be able to tell the fire was started, but not by what. If the guy wore gloves, had keys, or found an unlocked door or window, chances are he would never leave anything behind for us to find."

"I always say criminals aren't too bright anyway, that's why they are criminals and not criminalists," Arias laughed. "The State Department says he has a U.S. Passport in his own name so we are checking hotels in Nassau, the Bahamas to locate him. We'll keep in touch." With that Arias hung up the phone.

He stepped around the cubicle to Padilla's office and grinned at him. "Remember the soda can we handed Nyland to get a sample of his DNA? Well, it worked. Buck Martin said they found a match to the blood in the driveway where his car was parked. So we can prove without a doubt he was there."

Padilla handed Arias three sheets of paper. "Here's your portion of the list of hotels in Nassau. Let's see if we can find him."

Four hours later, Arias shouted over the cubicle "Bingo! We found him. He is at The Reef in Nassau. He checked in early the morning after the fire started with a lady friend. He used his own name and his U.S. Passport with a wad of cash. They think he's an upper-level executive with a Florida firm and he's spending dough like he makes it himself."

"We'd better let the DA know. He'll want to alert the Justice Department in Washington so they can start the paperwork. How did you leave your contact at the hotel?"

"Very friendly!" Arias said. "I asked the manager to give me a call if anything changes there. I didn't tell them what we want the creep for but he's assuming it is serious or we wouldn't be calling. He has friends in other hotels and knows we're looking for this guy. He promised to keep an eye on him for us. I told him to expect a visit from their police department soon so he's keeping a log of his comings and goings for me. Nice chap, that manager is. Real helpful."

"Give me the name and phone number, will ya? I will call it in to the District Attorney's office so they can forward it on to the Justice Department. We need to catch this guy before he decides to take off for somewhere else," Padillo told him.

Arias stepped back into his cubicle and scooped up his notes and handed them to his partner. "Now can we go to lunch? I'm starved."

"Let me call the DA with this information first. I'll meet you downstairs in five minutes. Where'd you want to go?"

Alice Smarte – with an 'e' – was the Deputy District Attorney assigned to the Arson Case against David Nyland. She was busy writing the complaint for the Justice Department in Washington when her phone rang. "Smarte here," she answered and listened. "Good detective work there, Officer Padilla. You are most helpful. Give me that address, phone number, and the manager's name if you don't mind. I'm preparing the complaint for Justice now, so we can get a push on this. We don't want this guy disappearing again."

Alice jotted down the information in her tight neat hand on one of her numerous yellow lined legal tablets. She set it down by her laptop. When she hung up the phone, she began filling the information in on the form she was preparing. She too had worked on several arson cases they suspected David Nyland of doing. She wanted him off the streets. This particular case was even closer to her heart. She owned a cabin north of Boulder she loved to visit on weekends to decompress from her day job. That cabin was probably a pile of smoking ashes right now. She hadn't been able to confirm that yet. If it was gone, she had a very personal reason to put David Nyland in prison for a long time. She'd heard there were also three confirmed deaths in the fire. It was still early in the game and the fire was raging on.

Officer Arias got to the office early the next day and stopped by the coffee pot in his unit for a cup of the hot black stuff to get his heart beating and ready for the day. He found a note on his desk the night guy left for him. He glanced at the pink slip of paper and the name jumped out at him. It was from the manager of The Reef Hotel in Nassau. He sipped his coffee before setting the cup on his desk and grabbing the phone. "Wonder what this is all about?" he thought as he waited for the hotel operator to come on the line. He asked for the manager by name and sat on hold another 15 seconds before hearing the man's cheery British accent.

"What can I do for you?" Arias questioned the man.

"I told you I'd give you a call if I heard anything on your man down here. I got a call early this morning from some chap, said he was from New York, asking about your guy and if he'd checked in. I've dealt with people all my life and see all kinds in the hotel business you know. There was just something about the guy that raised the hair on the back of my neck. I lied and told him no one by that name had checked into this hotel. Just the way he slammed down the phone in my ear put me off. I called some of my friends in the business down here, the ones I'd told you shared with me that you had been calling around. He's been calling all over the island it seems. None of us got a name, but I did get the caller ID number for you."

"Interesting," Arias pondered. "Wonder who this guy is and what he wants with Nyland. Give me the caller ID number you got, and I'll check it out. Thanks for the tip, man. We really appreciate it. Maybe I'll get to bring my bride to Nassau someday. I promise to look you up and buy you a drink." As Arias hung up the phone he heard Padilla sit down in his cubicle. He popped over and told him about the phone call.

Detective Padilla picked up his phone and called Alice Smarte at the DA's office. He filled her in on the call from the Bahamas his partner just had. "Someone is looking for our guy. I've already told you what Buck Martin, the Arson Investigator, told me about the building owner where the fire originated. That man has more money than brains. If he's got someone looking for Nyland, it could be he's trying to silence him so we can't trace the arson back to him. Should we be offering some kind of protection for Nyland if we want to get him back here for trial? Why don't you talk to the DA yourself and see what he thinks?"

Alice Smarte thought about that for a minute. The silence on the phone was deafening for Padilla. "Do you or your partner have a U.S. Passport?" she finally asked him.

"Yes, we both do," Padilla said quizzically. "Why do you ask?"

"Maybe we should send one or both of you to Nassau to keep an eye on Nyland while the Justice Department works their magic with the Bahamians. I need to talk to the DA and see what he thinks. Could either of you go if we need you?"

"Well, that would have to be cleared with the Department here first. But I'm sure we could get on a plane and spend some time tailing him if we need to. We have a man at the hotel we trust who can help us there," Padilla answered thoughtfully. He'd always wanted to take his wife on a trip to the Caribbean. He knew she wanted to go. How would she feel if he went with his partner and left her at home? She'd probably not take that well. He sighed.

"I'll get back to you as soon as I can. Thanks for the heads up." Alice Smarte hung up and dashed out of her office. If someone really was looking for Nyland in Nassau, it probably wasn't for a good purpose. She wanted to put that man in prison for this crime and several others that crossed her desk in the past few years.

CHAPTER NINETEEN

Hilda Jorgensen hugged Todd and thanked him again. She told him she needed to freshen up a bit and she would be out to see the other kids in a couple of minutes. Todd rejoined the others in the living room where the talk was all about the time they spent in the canyon and the terrifying ride Desperado led them on to get there. There was a lot of talk about what a hero Desperado was in the entire situation.

About a half hour later, while Hilda regaled the parents with her own tales of the adventure, the phone rang. Sharon answered it and listened for a bit, then spit out "No Comment!" and slammed the phone down. No sooner had she hung up than the phone rang again. Sharon answered it and repeated her earlier performance. The phone rang again. She looked over at Chris and mouthed "Your turn" silently.

Chris hurried to the kitchen phone and answered it. He listened for a few seconds and said "No Comment" and hung up. This time he waited until the phone call disconnected and took the phone off the hook and set it down on the counter.

Sharon looked at Chris and asked, "What are we going to do?"

Chris shrugged his shoulders and said, "I think I'll take a walk out and see what Chief Odom suggests. We can't keep our phone off the hook forever because other family members are trying to reach people here now. But we don't want to be swarmed by reporters either. Maybe the Chief has a suggestion. Just leave the phone off the hook until I get back."

Chris marched out of the mudroom and up the hill to the Command and Control unit of the Fire Department. He knocked on the door until someone inside invited him in. Chief Odom was on the phone with one of his Battalion Chiefs, so Chris waited. As soon as Chief Odom hung up, Chris explained about the reporters dogging them.

"Oh, I thought we might get a day off before this started," Odom told him. "I'm really sorry. Let me call my boss and see about a press conference. It's probably time for a public update on the fire anyway and we can use a couple of representatives from the parents at the conference. That would keep the reporters away from the kids and poor Hilda Jorgensen. I think, if we have it at the ranch next door, we might be able to keep them at bay for a while longer. Those poor kids need their family time right now. I'm assuming none of them need to see a doctor, right? How about the horses? Any of them injured during their expedition?"

Chris assured Chief Odom everyone made it through the ordeal with nothing more than a slight scratch and a few singed hairs. "That's excellent," the Chief said. "Let me make the call and I'll come to the house and talk to you and the other parents in about half an hour."

When Chris got back to his house, he called the parents together in the living room to discuss the news conference. None of them really wanted to participate, but Grandpa

Carnegie and George Reeves volunteered to stand with Chris. That would leave everyone else off the hook.

Chris looked at Walter Howard and said, "Walter, your family owns Prince Ali. He's the two and a half million dollar stallion. Those reporters are going to be rabid to know what's going on with him. Why don't you join the three of us at the news conference so Caroline and Becky don't have to? While we're all here, we should probably discuss those of you who need to drive back to California and when you want to leave. Because of what's going on here, we may want to stagger departures and set up a meeting place where you guys can join up down the road away from Boulder."

Discussion continued for a while in the living room with the adults. They decided to postpone the trip to California for that night rather than try to leave right after the News Conference. It was a 14-hour drive so they wanted a fresh start in the morning.

The nine older kids went to the barn to see their horses. The younger ones took advantage of Todd's video games in the playroom. Within an hour the adults had a plan for departure staggered 15 minutes apart with a meeting place along the road between Denver and Grand Junction, near the turnoff for Vail. That would be a good place to stop for fuel and something to eat before pressing on for California.

With plans in the works, the women turned to the kitchen to prepare the next meal. Sharon had a large well-stocked freezer and she took advantage of that planning ahead to feed such a large crowd. Hilda tried to pitch in too, but Sharon sat her on a stool at the kitchen island with a large cup of tea. Sharon was worried. Hilda looked very tired. She was able to engage in the discussions in the kitchen and kept the ladies laughing as she talked about the funny things that happened in that quiet canyon in the wilderness.

Chief Odom returned to the house with a time for the News Conference. His bosses would be there with several of the Battalion Chiefs so they could update the media on the progress of fire suppression. Fortunately, the weather was in their favor and the winds died down considerably. The fire was beginning to lay down overnight and progress was made.

Chris let Chief Odom know he, Walter Howard, George Reeves and Charles Carnegie would attend the conference. He told Chief Odom that George Reeves was local to the area and his son was among the youngsters caught up in the fire. Walter Howard was the owner of Prince Ali and Charles Carnegie's granddaughter was one of the kids from the canyon. Chief Odom briefly talked to the four men then rushed back to the Command and Control Unit with a promise that he would come to get the four and take them to the News Conference himself.

When the five men arrived in the Chief's car, the place was a madhouse. There were at least a hundred reporters from print and television with cameras and microphones waiting to pounce on anyone who could give them a soundbite. They crowded, pushing and shoving to the podium, shouting questions as the participants gathered there.

The State Fire Chief opened the News Conference himself. He introduced the firemen with him and began the briefing. The reporters weren't interested in fire updates at all. They continuously and rudely interrupted the man asking questions about the missing kids and their horses. He finally halted the conference briefly. "Gentlemen and ladies, we are here to update you on this wildfire that has already burned over 78,000 acres of woodland, destroyed homes and ranches and taken the lives of at least three people. We will get to the missing kids when we're done with our business. I won't be taking any questions about them until our briefing is done." With that, he introduced Chief Don Odom who took the microphone and explained how many firefighters were on the front lines, how much air support they had from Colorado and other states, where the active fire was burning at the moment, and what their plan for fighting the fire was. Chief Odom introduced his Battalion Chiefs, one at a time, and let them give their personal impressions from front-line experience. Once that portion of the conference was over, Chief Odom took the microphone again and introduced the four men with them. The reporters began screaming questions immediately. "How is Prince Ali?", "Did any of the kids get hurt?", "How is the old lady with them?", "Is Prince Ali going to perform again?", "How is little Becky Howard?", How did they survive in that canyon?", "How did they find a safe place?", "Did anyone get burned?"

Chris O'Neal couldn't speak. He had no idea how to talk over the questions and the uproar. George Reeves was also mute as was Walter Howard. Charles Carnegie, however, had numerous experiences with news conferences in his day. He'd worked on a number of celebrities during his time as a neurosurgeon and learned to deal with reporters wanting information on his patients. He looked at Chief Odom and raised his eyebrow. Chief Odom understood his cue and handed the microphone to Grandpa Carnegie.

"I'm Charles Carnegie, that's spelled C H A R L E S C A R N E G I E. My granddaughter, Maryann Wilcox, was one of the young people who sought refuge in the canyon with her horse. This fine gentleman on my left is Chris O'Neal – spelled C H R I S O' N E A L. He is a horse trainer and the owner of Cold Water Creek Ranch where several of the horses, including

Prince Ali, were trained. This gentleman to my right is George Reeves – spelled G E O R G E   R E E V E S. His son, Charlie was trapped in the canyon with my granddaughter. The gentleman to the right of him is Walter Howard – spelled W A L T E R H O W A R D. He is the owner of Prince Ali, the horse you are most familiar with. His daughter Becky was also trapped in the canyon with Prince Ali. We will be happy to answer your questions, but we need to do that one at a time. The reporters quieted down and looked more respectfully at Mr. Carnegie. He saw a hand raise from the group in front of him and he pointed to the woman. "What's your question ma'am?"

From that point, reporters raised their hands and respectfully asked their questions. George, Walter, and Chris stepped in and answered many of them. They told the story the kids told when they arrived back at the ranch. Walter assured them Prince Ali was in good shape and he would be competing again with his daughter. George told them about his night in the canyon with the kids before they walked out. Chief Odom explained how they were alerted to the kids' location by the recon helicopter pilot and how they dropped supplies in for them and the horses. He also explained how they had to bulldoze a path for them to get out of the canyon and back to the highway. He told them how many State and Federal agencies were involved in the rescue efforts. A couple of times, a reporter shouted his question over others speaking. Charles Carnegie stopped the conference to let him know they couldn't answer more than one question at a time. He was marvelous at maintaining control and keeping it civil and informative.

After 55 minutes of grueling questioning, everyone in front of the podium was exhausted and the questions finally ended. Chief Odom returned the four men to Cold Water Creek Ranch and resumed his own duties.

CHAPTER TWENTY

Alice Smarte waited her turn to see the District Attorney with great impatience. She sat in the chair outside of his office hugging her notes close to her chest. She crossed her legs and bobbed the upper one up and down in her angst. She thought about what the two police detectives had told her, both about the perp who probably burned down her weekend sanctuary and the man who probably hired him. She had a real dislike for both men.

The door to the District Attorney's office opened suddenly and Alice jerked to attention. She watched as one of her colleagues walked out into the lobby area and went straight to the elevator, pushing the down button. She jumped to her feet just as the D.A. stepped out to his secretary's desk.

"Sir, I'd like to have a word with you if you can," Alice spoke up. Beau Collier smiled at her. "Sure Alice. Come on in. I have a few minutes now."

Alice fiddled with her notes briefly before telling him the purpose of her meeting. "I'm not sure but I think there may be someone else looking for our guy in the Bahamas." She relayed the conversation she'd had with Arias a few minutes before. "Maybe we should send our detectives to Nassau to keep an eye on him while the Justice Department gets their paperwork together. My contact at the Justice Department told me the extradition procedure with the Bahamians is quick in the case of a murder so the Bahamian police will pick Mr. Nyland up and incarcerate him until we send someone to escort him back to Denver. I'd just like to be sure he gets back here. How would you feel about sending the detectives now?"

"Before I spend that much taxpayer money, I'd like to go over this with you again. Tell me why you are worried about Mr. Nyland in the first place, from the beginning," Collier asked.

Alice laid it all out for him including the fact someone was calling hotels all over Nassau looking for him without leaving a name. She'd looked up the caller ID given by the manager of The Reef in Nassau and it was a burner phone dumped at the Miami airport. Miami airport police found it. It had no fingerprints on it. All the phone numbers it dialed in the preceding six hours were five-star hotels in Nassau, Bahamas, none of which was more than three minutes long.

"How soon can you get our own cops on a plane?" Collier asked her. "I will get going on this end. I'll get Department permission to send them and have tickets sent over right away. You need to let those guys know they have a plane to catch."

Alice rushed back to her office and called Officer Padilla. She explained what she wanted them to do and told him plane tickets were on their way over by messenger. She jotted down the cell phone number of both Padilla and Arias for her files and called her contact at the Justice Department in Washington.

Officer Padilla explained the situation to his boss and he and Arias waited in the lobby for the plane tickets, then took off in separate cars for home to pack. They would meet at the ticket counter at the airport in 45 minutes. They had no time to spare.

David Nyland called downstairs to book a reservation at The Reef's fine dining room that evening at 7:00 p.m. The Concierge, who was also the evening Maître D' himself, took the call. He'd heard rumors from other staffers at the hotel what a good tipper Mr. Nyland was, so he showed him every courtesy possible. "I have just the table for you, sir. I will seat you at Table 7 which is one of the best in the house. I will personally seat and serve you and your guest this evening. Is there anything special I should have ready for you?"

Mr. Nyland muttered about celebrating something. The Concierge caught that right away. "Sir, I will have a bottle of our finest champagne chilled and ready for you when you get here. I'm looking forward to serving you."

The hotel manager, Wilson Vickers, looked over the restaurant bookings for the night late that afternoon. He saw the comment for Table 7 next to Mr. Nyland's 7:00 booking. He'd never seen the guy but knew there was interest in him from the American law enforcement people. He made himself a note to look in on him in the dining room. He also checked to be sure Table 18 was available and blocked it off for the night so no one else could reserve it. The manager heard from the front desk people what an interesting couple he and his lady friend were, and he had to see it for himself.

Mr. Vickers was at the fine dining room by 6:45 p.m. that evening and talked to guests as they checked in for their tables. Many of them he already knew from earlier encounters around the hotel. The wealthy people who frequented places like The Reef often had special requests that involved his approval for the staff. He always gave it but often wondered why such requests were made in the first place. He was standing inches from the podium when Mr. Nyland approached. He had his arm tucked around the elbow of one of the most beautiful women Mr. Vickers had ever seen.

"Nyland, party of two for 7:00 please," Nyland said to the Maître D'.

"Oh, of course, Mr. Nyland. Please come with me. I have your table ready," the Maître D' said graciously bowing just a bit.

"Please let me introduce myself," Mr. Vickers spoke up. "Actually, I have Table 18 ready for you. Our Table 7 is one of the best in the house, but Table 18 is the best. I'm Wilson Vickers, the hotel manager, sir. I'm pleased to have you as our guests. I've spoken to the chef. He recommends the chateaubriand with halibut or the steak and lobster as some of his best for tonight. I'll have your champagne delivered to Table 18 for you."

Vickers was taken aback by Nyland's appearance. It was as described. He was very tall and painfully thin. He wore plaid Bermuda shorts topped by a brightly printed Hawaiian shirt with his feet tucked into white socks and open-toed sandals. His head was bald in a circle on top surrounded by frizzy red hair that stuck out all over. His small sharp eyes perched above a nose that looked more like a bird's beak. His Adam's apple climbed and dropped up and down his scrawny neck every time he spoke or swallowed. The woman with him was the exact opposite. She wore a lovely little black dress that hugged her curves. She wore delicate diamond studs in her ears and a lovely diamond solitaire necklace on a gold chain around her neck. Her thick, glossy dark hair was piled up in an elegant updo the showed off her bare shoulder and graceful neck. The only other ornament on her was the very large diamond on the ring finger of her left hand. Just the way she carried it, Mr. Vickers deduced the ring was new.

As Vickers led them to the private room enclosing Table 18, he commented on the new diamond ring. "Is this perhaps the reason for the celebration tonight?" he asked them.

The woman blushed. "Please call me Jessica," she said. "Soon to be Jessica Nyland."

David Nyland stood a bit taller and threw what little chest he had out in pride. "Yes, she agreed to marry me this afternoon."

Mr. Vickers congratulated the couple and made his exit as the Maître D' came in with the champagne. He left the dining room shaking his head. "It takes all kinds," rumbled around in his thoughts while he stifled a chuckle and tried to remain dignified until he could have some privacy for a good laugh. He couldn't imagine what the police department in Denver, Colorado wanted with that clown in his dining room.

The Maître D' seated a high-level executive with a major broadcasting network in New York and his wife at Table 7. They came to Nassau two or three times a year for a week to decompress. They always spent plenty of money at The Reef during their visits.

Earlier that afternoon, the tall man got a call on his new burner cell phone. "Yeah?" he answered. The voice on the other end spoke quickly. "He's having dinner tonight at The Reef's fine dining room, Table 7." The caller clicked off.

The tall man found a restaurant supply house in Nassau and bought himself a wait-staff uniform to match those worn at The Reef. He told the clerk he'd ruined his and needed it because he was called in on his day off and couldn't wait for his uniform to be cleaned. He paid for it in cash and went back to his hotel. He pulled on a pair of surgical gloves and did a little work at the desk in his hotel room. He finished up and put a black metal rectangle carefully in a plastic box. He attached a special tape around the box, so he could un-tape the ends and re-tape them. He put on the uniform and slipped the box into his pocket. He hailed a cab from the entrance of his hotel and got out a block from The Reef. He took the back alley to the rear kitchen door and waited. One of the regular staffers came out hauling a bag of garbage to the trash bin. The tall man slipped in the back door. He looked around for a few minutes watching the staff before stepping over and grabbing a pot of hot coffee. He pulled a fresh white dish towel over his arm and checked the table map on his way into the dining room. It was early so there were few diners in the room. He located Table 7 and fussed with the tablecloth for a minute. It only took him seconds to remove the plastic box from his pocket and tape it to the underside of the table. The timer was already set for 7:30 p.m. He added the extra time in case his target was a few minutes late. If he was on time, he should be in the middle of his main course at 7:30. He offered fresh coffee to a couple of diners before heading back to the kitchen. He dropped off the dish towel and the coffee pot on his way to the back door. He slipped out the door and down the alley, stripping off the gloves, coat and bow tie which he dropped in different dumpsters in the alley. He disappeared down the main street that ran past The Reef and walked several blocks before hailing a cab to get back to his hotel.

At 7:30 p.m. The Reef dining room rocked from the explosion. People were thrown from their chairs, tables overturned, glasses and plates of food crashed to the floor and shattered. Windows blew out sending showers of glass out on the people on the patio by the pool. The concussion caused momentary deafness for people in the room who survived. The two guests seated there were thrown several feet away from the table. A gentleman walking past Table 7 on his way to the men's room at the time of the blast was thrown ten feet away. Injuries were numerous. People screamed and scrambled to get out of the dining room. The hotel was complete pandemonium in seconds. Because of the blast, people racing to get away took the stairwells rather than elevators. People stumbled and fell. Others fell on top of them. Smoke from the explosion poured out the broken windows in the dining room and guests outside feared the hotel was on fire. David Nyland and Jessica rushed out of their private dining room. He pulled her through the kitchen to the rear alley because everyone else seemed to be going the other way.

CHAPTER TWENTY-ONE

After the News Conference, everyone at Cold Water Creek Ranch finalized their plans for those leaving in the morning for California. The men and boys handled the extra livestock remaining on the ranch because of the evacuations from the fire. Many of the horses had already been picked up and taken home or relocated to more permanent housing elsewhere in the valley. The women prepared the last group meal they would share at the ranch with the help of the girls, some of which also helped entertain the younger children.

Late that afternoon, trailers were brought to the ranch and packed for departure with anything that had been taken out for use during their stay. Once the packing was completed and their evening meal cleaned up after, those who were staying in the ski lodges down the road left to get some much-needed sleep before departure in the morning.

The barn was quiet at last. Desperado's stall was right next to Prince Ali's. In fact, there was a chain holding Desperado's stall door closed that was attached to the front bars on Ali's stall with a padlock. Chris had finally found a device Desperado couldn't unlock to keep him in his stall and safe at night.

"You asleep, Ali" Desperado whispered through the bars of his stall.

"Naw, just digesting my dinner and thinking about getting some shut-eye," Ali answered.

"What's going to happen now?" Desperado asked. *"I know you guys from California are going home tomorrow. You have a long haul. I just worry about our brothers and sisters up in the northern territory. Hope they get that fire out soon. It sure burned up a lot of areas where the wild creatures live. I spent a lot of time when I was younger watching the wild things in the woods. I learned a lot from them. Now they don't have a home if they even survived. I felt sorry for the mamma bear and her two cubs that nearly tripped me. Where is she going to go and feed her babies?"*

"I was going to ask you about that. How did you know about the place you took us? That was quite a way off the usual trail we ride. Not that I'm complaining. It was fortunate you could get us all there and in one piece. And there was fresh water and some grass to eat." Ali said.

"When I was young and lived at home with Jan and Hilda, I used to play tricks on Jan and get my stall door open at night. At first, I just wandered around the property until he found me and put me back in my paddock. It was lots of fun. As I got a little older I got a little bolder and started wandering out behind the fence. I found deer out there. I just watched them. I learned a lot from them. They will talk to you, but only if you don't scare them away first,"

"Yes, I talked to some deer once myself," Ali told him. *"I was hungry and saw some of the females with their babies eating and asked if I could join them. They were wary but friendly when I assured them I am a grass eater like they are."*

"I met a young female in the woods. Her name is Blaze because she has an interesting white mark on her face. Deer don't usually

have white markings after they shed their baby coats, you know. Well, she was a tiny little thing, but she and I became friends and used to hang out and wander around together. I think she liked being with me because I was bigger than her and maybe it made her feel safer. You know the mountain lions eat deer, don't you?" Desperado explained.

"That's probably why they are so wary and suspicious of strangers," Ali said. "I had a mountain lion jump on me in the woods. That scared the heck out of me and her fangs and her claws hurt bad. I still have scars from that. Fortunately, she met the wrong side of my back shoes and she didn't hurt me so badly I couldn't get away from her. I'm a full-grown horse. I can't imagine how scary those big cats would be to a tiny little deer."

"Yeah, I feel really bad because Blaze is the one that showed the canyon to me in the first place. She took me there and made me promise on my word of honor I would never tell anyone else about the place. The deer use it when they need refuge. There's fresh water and some food for them and it's their secret place to hide. I broke my promise to Blaze when I took the horses and the kids into that canyon. If any of the deer sought refuge in the canyon and found us there, they wouldn't have come in. I may have cost lives, hopefully not Blaze or her children," Desperado admitted sadly.

"Look, Desperado, you did what you knew would save us and our humans. We all need to thank Blaze for showing you that canyon. If we hadn't gone there we might have ended up burned up like the forest around us did. Hopefully, you will see Blaze again and can explain it to her. I'm so grateful we could save my Becky and your Todd and all the others. If you do ever see her again, thank her for me. I will remember what you told me. I will always hold the deer in the highest regard because she saved our lives," Ali told him.

"*Thank you for keeping my secret. Some of the humans are saying I'm a hero for taking the group into that canyon. I wouldn't have known about it except for my tiny deer friend named Blaze. She's the real hero in this story, not me.*"

Ali snorted. "*Don't discount yourself, my friend. If you had not made friends with Blaze, you wouldn't have known there was a place of refuge to go. You are still a hero to me and the others. What other horse do you know of makes friends with the wild creatures, so they share their secrets with you? None that I've ever talked to. None I've ever heard about either.*"

"*I guess I'm really feeling bad because I broke my word to her and that may have cost the lives of other deer. There's nothing I can do about it now except hope Blaze will forgive me and still be my friend.*"

Ali shook his head. "*Desperado, you saved the lives of nine other horses including your own mother. On top of that, you saved the lives of 10 humans. You saved Hilda and your best friend, Todd. What else were you to do? You need to stop worrying and get some sleep.*"

"*Yeah. Yeah. I know. But then I start thinking about that other problem I talked to you about before. I don't want to get shipped off to some gosh-forsaken frozen barn in Michigan or some sweaty place in South Carolina and never see my family or Todd again. It would even be worse if Mr. Babcock, the bunny-kicker man bought me. He scares me if you want the truth. If anything happens to Hilda, that's probably what will happen to me. Hilda's children won't want me around and they will want as much money for me as they can get. They won't care I want to stay with Todd. They look at me and see dollar signs and that's all. I've screwed up and made things worse by trying my best with Todd when we compete. If I goofed up a class on purpose that Todd was riding me in, I'd never be able to live with myself. But*" doing well in the class puts me out of his range. Chris and Sharon work really hard with other people's horses on this ranch but they don't have the money to buy a champion horse for their son. The whole situation just kind of sucks."

"Desperado, you need to lighten up! You are going to worry yourself into an early grave," Ali snorted again. "Please, believe me, you are in good hands. The people around you are good people and sometimes they do things that will surprise you. Look at Maryann and La Duquesa. Her grandparents showed up out of nowhere and ended up giving La Duquesa to Maryann as her very own horse. How's that for a happy ending? People really do the right things sometimes. Everyone knows how much Todd loves you and they know how much you love Todd. Give 'em some time! Now, I need to get some sleep. Stop worrying and get some yourself."

CHAPTER TWENTY-TWO

Detectives Padillo and Arias were on their flight to Miami when the explosion at The Reef in Nassau occurred. Their cell phones were turned off during the flight so they had no idea until they checked their phones in the Miami terminal while waiting for their flight to Nassau. It was nearing midnight when they arrived in Miami and they had a two-hour wait because of their international destination. They wouldn't arrive until early the next morning.

Arias was the first one to see the message from their boss. Padillo was dialing his phone to return a call from Mr. Vickers at The Reef. Arias called the Detective Watch Commander back while Padillo looked serious, then in shock while he listed to Mr. Vickers on his phone.

"You called?" Arias said when his boss answered his cell phone in Denver.

"Yea. I did. Where are you and Padillo right now?" his boss asked sharply,

"We just got to Miami, sir. Is something wrong? Padillo is talking to someone who left him a message and he doesn't look too happy."

"I talked to Mr. Vickers myself. He was trying to reach you two but you were on the flight. There was an explosion at The Reef tonight. There were several people killed and many injured in the blast. Many more people were injured in the panic following the explosion. The scene is in chaos at the moment. I gave Mr. Vickers your flight details. He's sending a car for you. You and your partner need to get to that hotel right away. Mr. Vickers thinks someone was trying to kill our David Nyland. He has personal knowledge he needs to share with you. Mr. Nyland and his new fiancé were not injured, at least not that anyone knows, but they have disappeared. We need to find them!"

Padillo tugged at Arias's shoulder just as Arias hung up his cell phone. "Who were you talking to?" he asked.

"I was just talking to our boss. Apparently, Mr. Vickers talked to him not too long ago. We're walking into a mess in the Bahamas."

"Yeah, that's what I got from Alice Smarte in the DA's office. She told me the Bahamian Police Department is waiting for us in Nassau and will go with us to The Reef to help sort the mess there out. We've got to find Nyland and we need to find him fast. Someone is trying to eliminate him. The Police Department there is watching the airports closely for departures. They are detaining people who don't check out like regular tourists or businessmen. Maybe their net will catch our fish too."

"Did you get any other calls while we were on the flight?" Arias asked.

"Just the one from my very unhappy wife," Padillo said with a frown. "She's always wanted to go to the Bahamas. Now I'm on my way there but I'm taking you with me instead of her. She's a bit grumpy about that. When we get this case solved, I may pull some money out of the credit union and buy two tickets for us. You know what they say….Unhappy Wife – Unhappy Life."

"Yeah. Pauline wasn't too happy about it either," Arias told him.

The two detectives strolled around the Miami terminal until they found a decent place for a meal. They finished up in time to board the flight to Nassau.

It was a short flight to the Bahamas, less than an hour. When they arrived, two members of the local police department stood holding signs with their names on them. They immediately talked to them and were hustled through customs ahead of the other passengers from Miami and whisked into a patrol car which sped them directly to The Reef Hotel as the sun came up. The Bahamian officers didn't have much to say during the entire process. When they arrived at the hotel, the police cruiser was parked in front of the hotel and Padillo and Arias were escorted into Mr. Vickers office on the ground floor in the maze of offices behind the front desk of the hotel. The police escorts took up a position outside of the office on either side of the door.

Mr. Vickers immediately stood when Padillo and Arias were ushered into his office. "Detectives Padillo and Arias, I assume?" he asked.

"Yes, I'm Detective Padillo and this is my partner, Detective Arias," Padillo answered as Mr. Vickers came around his desk and stuck out his right hand to shake with the new arrivals.

"I'm very happy to meet you. You've come at a bad time but we're certainly glad you are here," Mr. Vickers said to them as he vigorously shook their hands. "These other gentlemen are with the Bahamian government and," pointing at the only man in uniform in the room, "this is our Chief of Police, Chief Oxley."

Once the introductions were completed and Detective Padillo and Arias were seated around the conference table with the others, Detective Padillo asked, "Can you tell me what happened here in as much detail as you have right now?" Padillo and Arias took out their notebooks and pens ready to begin taking notes.

"At precisely 7:30 p.m., a bomb of significant force exploded under Table 7 in our fine dining room. There were several immediate fatalities from the explosion and numerous other injuries from moderate to severe caused by the explosion. The ceiling in the dining room may be falling in which will drop hotel rooms from the second floor into that room and may further damage the structure of this hotel. The resulting panic caused a number of other severe injuries in the stampede to evacuate that room and others nearby. There were additional moderate to severe injuries to guests on the patio by the pool area. The dining room windows overlooked that area and were blown out showering guests with flying glass. Currently, the Princess Margaret Hospital, Doctors Hospital, and the Bahamas Medical Center are treating patients to their capacity. Several critical patients were airlifted to Miami and are being treated at Mercy Hospital, the University of Miami Hospital and Jackson Memorial Hospital. The coroner has been here and removed several of the fatalities to our local morgue. I don't believe we have a complete count of the injuries or fatalities yet. Our engineering department is looking at the structural soundness of the hotel right now. I should have their report within 30 minutes," Mr. Vickers said as he checked his watch. "This has not been a good day."

"May I ask you why you believe the explosion was intended for Mr. Nyland?" Padillo asked.

"Like I told you on the phone, many of my people here at the hotel have spoken to me about that guest and his tendency to drop money around. They also talked about his strange appearance and how beautiful his companion is. I checked the reservation list for the fine dining room about 4:00 this afternoon, as is my custom, and found his name on the list for 7:00 p.m. Table 7 was being held for him and his lady friend. I blocked off Table 18 in the dining room, which is a private room rather than a table in the open and joined the Concierge at the desk to check him in, strictly out of curiosity, mind you."

"Uh, huh," mumbled Arias. "What happened next?" He was scribbling in his notebook as he spoke and barely raised his eyes to catch a glance at Mr. Vickers.

"Mr. Nyland and his friend, who is now his fiancé by the way, were right on time. The Concierge was going to show them to Table 7 but I interrupted and personally showed them to Table 18 instead. I had noticed a large diamond on Jessica's left hand, she introduced herself to me, and I mentioned that must be the reason for their celebration that night. She told me she would soon be Mrs. Nyland and he told me he'd just asked her that afternoon," Mr. Vickers continued.

"Why do you believe someone was targeting Mr. Nyland directly," asked Padillo as he scribbled notes in his notebook.

"Like I said, they had reservations for 7:00 that night at Table 7. I changed them to Table 18 at the last minute. Table 7 is the one that blew up. I can't think but someone must have wanted him dead," Mr. Vickers answered. "I seriously don't believe anyone wanted the couple seated at Table 7 dead. He's a high-level executive for a major broadcasting network out of New York. They come down here a couple of times a year for a week to relax. They are well liked here in Nassau, and especially well liked at my hotel. They are very gracious people, good tippers, and easy to talk to. I can't make myself believe someone wanted to do that to those nice people."

"Who had access to your reservation system? Who would know that Mr. Nyland had a reservation that night and would be seated at Table 7?" Arias asked.

"Anyone on my staff would if it was important to know. Our reservation system is easy for the staff to access. When I talked to the Concierge who made the reservation, he said he booked the table for them at the second best table in the house hoping for some of the tips Mr. Nyland was known to hand out among the staff. They don't usually reserve Table 18 unless it is for a VIP of some note. I blocked that table out myself when I looked over the reservations for the night and saw Mr. Nyland's name for Table 7."

"Okay. We know Mr. Nyland made a reservation for dinner in the fine dining room here at the hotel for 7:00 p.m. We know your concierge bumped him up to Table 7 in the hopes he'd make a better tip that night and he wrote that in the reservation. You saw the reservation and blocked Table 18 off but didn't change the reservation chart until Mr. Nyland and his lady friend showed up to check in for dinner. You moved him to Table 18 yourself. At 7:30 p.m. Table 7 blew up and created a lot of destruction here at the hotel. Is that correct?" Detective Padilla asked, raising his head from his notebook and looking across the table at Mr. Vickers.

"Yes, that's all correct as I know it," Mr. Vickers said.

"Has anyone seen Mr. Nyland or his girlfriend since the blast?" Padillo asked him.

"That's the odd thing. Everyone in the room ran out the double doors into the corridor to the hotel lobby and exited through the front doors to the parking lot. Many guests ran down the stairwells because they were afraid the hotel was on fire and wanted to get out of here quickly. I've not spoken to a single person who saw Mr. Nyland or his girlfriend. They were very distinctive. If you saw them, you wouldn't forget them," Mr. Vickers answered.

"How was that? Can you give me a description of the couple?" Arias asked.

"Mr. Nyland is about six feet three or four inches tall and weighs approximately one hundred seventy pounds. He is very tall and very thin. He was dressed in plaid Bermuda shorts and wore a loud print, loose Hawaiian shirt over that. He wore plain white socks and sandals. He has red frizzy hair with a large bald spot on the top of his head, a prominent Adam's apple, and a nose that looks more like a bird's beak than a nose. It's pointed and overhangs his lip somewhat. He's really rather goofy looking. His lady friend, Jessica, on the other hand, is a beautiful woman about five feet five inches tall, maybe one hundred twenty pounds, and in all the right places. She has dark brown hair that was put up for that night. She needs very little makeup to look beautiful. She was wearing a close-fitting short black dress that showed off all of her curves. She had diamond earrings and a small diamond neckless on. The only other jewelry she wore was a very large diamond ring on the ring finger of her left hand. Like I said, if anyone saw those two together they would not forget them."

"If you were to speculate, where do you think they would go to hide?" Padilla asked.

"If I were them, I'd probably try to charter a boat to get me off this island," Vickers suggested. "Their room has not been entered since they left to come downstairs for dinner. I checked the electronic lock on their suite door. They couldn't have taken much with them but what they were wearing and they would stand out like a sore thumb anywhere."

"That answers another one of my questions, then," Arias said. "I wondered if they'd been able to get back into their room. Are you sure they didn't?"

"Absolutely sure," Vickers said. "Our key system records every entry and exit. They have not returned to their suite since the explosion."

"Did Mr. Nyland use the lock box in the hotel to store anything that you know of, like maybe part of the cash he brought with him?" Padillo asked.

"Actually, no," answered Mr. Vickers. "That's also pretty odd. He always seems to have plenty of money on him because he peeled off American Twenty Dollar bills like crazy around here. One of the maids got an American Hundred Dollar bill as a tip. She had to exchange it here at the hotel. The other odd thing about the man was that he seemed a bit thick around the middle. I wonder if he was wearing a money belt of some kind under that Hawaiian shirt. Now that you mention it, I'm guessing he was," Mr. Vickers mused. "That would explain his odd shape under his crazy mismatched clothes."

Padillo looked over his notes then looked at the Chief of Police. "Chief Oxley, what's your take on this?"

The Police Chief scratched his chin, obviously thinking about the situation. "My guess is this couple have their money with them and they are going to try and get off this island as quickly as they can. I have my people working with the fishing charter people now so they don't slip off the island by sea. If they have money with them, they've probably already changed their clothes so they won't look like they did at 7 p.m. last night. We are also watching the airports, both public and private ones to make sure they don't charter a flight anywhere. That should box them in on this island. Mr. Vickers is well connected among the hoteliers here so I'm sure he can get the word out to them that we are looking for this couple. Mr. Nyland must have figured out the same thing we did. Someone is trying to kill him. Maybe that someone is the same person who hired him for the arson job you two are looking for him to solve as well. If someone is trying to kill him to keep him silent, we need to take him into custody as fast as we can. We will put him right in our lock-up, surrounded by guards. You can talk to him while he is under our protection. I understand your Justice Department has already made inquiries about him to our government. We know you want to take him back to the United States so he can stand trial for Arson, Murder, and Destruction of Property. We'll work with your State Department people as soon as we take him into our custody."

"Sounds to me like we are all on the same page here," Detective Padillo said. "What can my partner and I do to help?"

CHAPTER TWENTY-THREE

Stephanie Underwood was terrified. She accepted a lot of American money from the man on the phone. She answered the phone for her boss, Mr. Vickers. When she told the caller he was not available the man sounded dejected. He told her he was trying to confirm his friend had checked into the hotel because he planned to surprise him. She fell for it. She asked him who his friend was and checked the register. She confirmed David Nyland and a female guest were checked into The Reef Hotel. The caller thanked her profusely. He seemed genuine to Stephanie at the time. He asked her for her address so he could leave her a little something as a thank you for her help. He told her to check her mailbox when she got home. She found a large package in her mailbox. She and her husband opened it together and joyfully tossed American bills around the room while they dreamed how they would spend all that lovely money.

It was enough to put a nice down-payment on a home with a view of the ocean in the nicer part of town. It was enough to buy a new car. It was enough to buy her husband a new boat for his charter business. The only problem was they couldn't convert it to local currency all at once. It would have to be exchanged over a period of time or she would have to answer some tough questions from the authorities. While her husband was very happy with the prospects of spending the money, she was not so sure. She thought about that and it was beginning to make her nervous.

She got another call from the man the morning before the explosion. He asked her if she found the gift he left for her. She told him she had and had not expected the gift to be so much. He assured her he was very grateful for her help. He told her there was a lot more where that had come from and passed it off as the least he could do for her help. He asked her to find out what David Nyland was up to. She'd checked the reservation sheets and found nothing for him. She suggested the man give her his phone number and she would call him if she found anything later in the day. She checked the reservation sheets after lunch and saw Mr. Nyland had a reservation for that evening at 7:00 p.m. in the fine dining room at The Reef. The reservation noted he was to be seated at Table 7. She called the number the mystery man left her and gave him that information.

She'd gone home last night after work not thinking one thing more about it until the news broadcast on TV said there had been an explosion at her hotel. She made her way back to the hotel immediately to see what she could do to help. The entire hotel was pandemonium. She made her way to her desk in front of Mr. Vickers' office before she heard the explosion was in the fine dining room and Table 7 had blown up, killing that nice executive and his wife. Suddenly she knew what she had done! She went into shock but she couldn't tell anyone at all. She had to hold herself together or give herself away. She was responsible for the deaths of several people and injuries to many more. She wasn't even sure the hotel would survive.

There was speculation that portions of the hotel may have to be rebuilt because of structural damage. She was responsible for all of this! What was she to do?

Stephanie sat at her desk and fielded calls for Mr. Vickers. He was called to different parts of the hotel to aid guests or staff during the crisis. She handled the calls she could and forwarded the ones she couldn't to his portable radio. She knew before anyone else about the American Policemen coming from Denver, Colorado. Stephanie had never been off the island before and struggled to remember high school geography to guess where Denver was in relation to her island.

Then the two gentlemen from the government and the Chief of Police arrived to see Mr. Vickers before the Americans got there. Mr. Vickers stopped at her desk and asked her to get them coffee and something from the pastry chef in the kitchen to eat. Mr. Vickers had not been home all night. He looked weary.

While the Americans were meeting with Mr. Vickers, the Police Chief and the representatives of the Bahamian government, she got another call from the American voice on the phone. She wanted to throw up and hang up the phone and run home but she didn't. "What do you want this time?" she snapped at him. "Haven't you done enough damage?"

"I do what I'm paid to do," said the man on the phone. "You, on the contrary, gave me bad information. I was very specific with you. I asked you where David Nyland would be and you told me. Now I find that your information was not accurate. Have you thought about what you will do without a husband?"

Stephanie was in mortal terror. Was this voice on the phone now threatening her? What was she going to do now? What could she do now? She pulled herself together and asked, "What do you want from me?"

"Do you know if David Nyland has been found? Is he wounded and in the hospital? If so, which one? I need to know now!" the voice on the phone said with emphasis on the word "now".

Stephanie was shaking so hard she could barely hold the phone. She steeled herself before she answered the man. "Not that I know of. Mr. Vickers told me no one has seen him or his companion since the explosion. They did not come out the front of the hotel with the other guests. We don't know where he is. There are policemen here from Colorado trying to find him now that they know you are trying to kill him. Yes, they figured that all out already. You might want to lay low yourself. They are looking for you too. Murder is a capital crime here in the Bahamas."

"Thank you, Stephanie. You've been very helpful," the voice said before hanging up the phone. Stephanie shook and began to cry. She was responsible for this horror. What was she going to do?

The tall man had it all figured out. David Nyland took a job from Henry Babcock. He was supposed to burn down four trees. Instead, he caused the second largest forest fire in the history of Colorado, burning more than 91,000 acres with an untold number of homes included. The damage was severe and not over yet. When the spring thaw began in the mountains and water rushed over hills denuded of foliage, mudslides could take whatever was left standing. He'd been sent to eliminate David Nyland. He knew full well Mr. Babcock would send someone to eliminate him too.

He decided to act like any normal tourist. He brought his scuba gear with him because he wanted to look like a tourist when he arrived. He would charter a boat for scuba diving. He wanted to explore the canyons beyond the reefs circling the island. He actually loved diving so this would be an easy diversion for him.

He hired a boat to take him to the reef off the coast of the island. He was the only passenger on the boat that day. He paid extra for that privilege. It was just him and the captain of the boat. He told the captain he would dive alone and brought several spare oxygen tanks with him when he loaded his gear on the boat the morning after the bombing at The Reef. He was pre-occupied during the cruise to the spot he wanted to dive on. He was trying to figure out his next move. He knew Mr. Babcock most definitely knew he failed in his assignment. That kind of mistake was fatal for the one who made it. He had to stay on the island for a few days and maintain his tourist appearance before he could safely leave. He knew all flights off the Island were being watched. Where did he want to go? Should he try to go back to the States or should he head for Europe? South America? The Orient? Could he lose himself in Australia? He needed to make a plan and make it quickly. He decided a long private dive would help clear his head so he could make that decision and plan for his future.

When the boat engine suddenly shut down, he jerked himself back to his present location and began tugging his dive suit on. He pulled on his breathing gear, put his dive computer on his left wrist and pulled flippers over his dive boots.

"I won't be too long," he told the Captain just before he slipped beneath the smooth clear water. He remembered why he loved diving as he began swimming across the top of the coral reef with it's brightly colored fish and coral animals. He concentrated on the beauty of the underwater world for a while before noticing a canyon beyond the reef. He checked his dive computer and it said he had plenty of time left to give it a view. He surveyed the canyon and noticed a cave down the undersea cliff that wasn't too far down. He swam down to explore it.

The cave mouth was wide enough for three divers across and two divers high. It wasn't too deep but there appeared to be a few aquatic creatures in there he wanted to take a good look at. He didn't realize he brushed against an outcropping of rock on the way into the cave. It sliced through one of his air hoses like a razor. A trail of bubbles from the rip in the hose followed him inside the cave. He was losing oxygen fast. Without a buddy around to notice it, he failed to discover the error. When he turned around to exit the large chamber, he finally noticed the large bubble formed on the roof of the cave by his escaping oxygen. He blanched at the sight and swam outside the cave quickly.

He knew he had at least one mandatory three minute stop to make on his way to the surface to prevent nitrogen bubbles from forming in his tissues, a condition called "the bends" in dive language. They could kill him. He hoped he had enough oxygen left in his tank and swam to the reef again. He was still too far down to reach the surface when his oxygen ran completely out. He fumbled with his dive weights but could not get them loose enough to drop them as he struggled to stave off unconsciousness. He lost that battle and the weights temporarily held his body on the reef. As he lost his battle with the sea, the last thing that ran through his mind was his original instructor's voice telling him it was a fool's errand to dive alone.

He was dead long before his body surfaced and washed up on one of the most beautiful beaches on the island.

CHAPTER TWENTY-FOUR

The morning came early for families in lodges down the highway from Cold Water Creek Ranch. The first lights went on a 2:30 a.m. The final packing of personal items was completed. Everyone got dressed for the drive. The first vehicles drove through the ranch entrance by 2:45 a.m. Younger children were excited about the drive for the moment.

The adults were worried about making a clean get-away. Reporters had been hanging around the gates of the ranch from early morning until late evening hoping to see one of the kids or Hilda and get a chance to talk to them directly. One visitor to the ranch had dropped the cougar story on them and they wanted more. They were like sharks who smelled blood in the water – constantly circling.

It was decided last night that those headed for California would leave one at a time in 15- minute intervals so they wouldn't attract attention. There was a meeting place set up at a freeway exit near Vail, Colorado. If you looked North from that exit you could see Vail Mountain and the resorts there. On the other side of the road was a gas station and nice restaurant. It was the perfect place to meet, add fuel, check on the horses and have breakfast. Their drive would be through Boulder and onto Denver and continuing to their pre-planned exit.

Ginny Hartley talked to Walter and Caroline Howard during the planning discussion. She invited them to stay at Hartley Ranch for the night instead of driving the extra two hours to San Juan Capistrano. Thinking about the fourteen to fifteen-hour drive across the desert, Walter agreed readily to the stopover. Maryann and Becky hatched their own scheme. Becky would spend that night with Maryann. Her parents could pick her up the next morning on their way home.

Hilda spent most of the night baking batches of her famous chocolate chip cookies for the trip. She got up early to make coffee, hot chocolate, and bagels for the departing families. She hugged each one of the youngsters and their parents as they left, pushing bags of cookies in their hands as they piled into the vehicles for departure.

The first truck and trailer turned onto the highway south at 3:30 a.m. The next vehicle followed them at 3:45 a.m. and they kept to their schedule of 15-minute intervals. Those in vehicles without trailers squeezed between the trucks. Everyone found the exit at Vail by 7:45 a.m. in perfect time for breakfast. It was still cool outside at that altitude but the day was sunny so most of the group had breakfast on the restaurant patio. They had not seen a reporter since the night before so the parents could finally relax and enjoy the beautiful day.

The balance of the trip to Hartley Ranch was uneventful. Younger children fell asleep, lulled by the motion of the vehicles. They woke at every fuel stop and helped feed and water the horses, generally getting wet in the process. Lunch was picked up and eaten on the road as they drove through Colorado, Utah, Nevada and the California desert. The trucks, trailers, and SUVs drove through the gates of Hartley Ranch close to 8:00 that night. Everyone on the trip was exhausted and the younger kids were cranky. Horses unloaded quickly. Gear was piled in heaps in the barn to be put away the next day. Mike Hartley and his foreman were there to help out so everyone could get on home. There were no reporters in view as the last vehicle drove out the gate of Hartley ranch. Unfortunately, that didn't last long.

Walter and Caroline woke early the next morning to the smell of freshly brewed coffee. They had a restful night and looked forward to getting home at long last. They pulled on their clothes and headed for the kitchen.

Mike was pouring himself a cup of coffee when Walter and Caroline walked into the kitchen. "Guess what?" he told them. "We have company outside."

"Really?" Walter asked. "Who's here?"

"Maybe we should ask whose not here," Mike said. "I was about to head to the barn when I noticed all the people behind our gate. They have TV crews out there. They are asking about Prince Ali and Becky."

Caroline sighed, "I'm so sorry, Mike. I know you don't like all this fuss."

"We might as well get it over with, then," Walter muttered. "I'll go out and see what we need to do to get rid of them." He took his coffee and walked out the back door.

Caroline's cell phone rang just as the back door shut behind Walter. She looked at her phone and realized it was a call from their home in San Juan Capistrano. She listened for a minute. "We'll try to get that taken care of here this morning, Espie. Please let Luis know we are going to meet with the reporters here. We'll see you in a couple of hours." She shook her head as she tucked her phone in her back pocket. "Our housekeeper, Espie, says they are swarming around our place too and getting to be a problem for Luis, our groundsman. Maybe if we just talk to them here they will leave us in peace for a while."

"Good luck with that!" Mike said sarcastically. "They want their story. Ali is pretty high-profile now since that last incident. It really is a good story. Nine kids and an old woman trapped in a canyon with ten horses during a wildfire. I'd probably be interested in that one myself." He chuckled.

"Let's see what Walter says after he talks to them," Caroline said. "Maybe we can get this done now so we can get on with our lives and get the fuss over with." She sat down at the kitchen table with her coffee. Ginny came down the hallway and joined them in the kitchen. The three of them chatted nervously while they waited for Walter.

Walter came back to the house a few minutes later. "Someone at the ranch, not one of us, said something to the reporters in Colorado about the cougar incident. The people outside related that to the attack Prince Ali suffered and they want to hear all about it. They really want to interview the kids who were in the canyon and see Prince Ali for themselves. We might have a chance to put this issue behind us if we let them talk to Brody, Maryann, and Becky. What do you all think?"

"You know, when Prince Ali was discovered here, we were swarmed by the media. Ginny was still down your place in San Juan Capistrano. It was just me and Brody here. He did a pretty good job of handling their questions. Maryann was with him part of the time and they did fine. We could let them talk to Brody, Maryann, and Becky, show them Ali and Quesa and the other horses and get this over with," Mike suggested. "The kids are in good shape and so are the horses. It was an adventure for them, but no one got hurt. We're really lucky."

When the adults agreed, Ginny called Rose Wilcox, Maryann's mother, and told her what was going on. She and the Carnegie's, Maryann's grandparents, would bring the two girls. Brody came in for breakfast and heard the news himself. He had breakfast while Mike, Caroline, and Ginny had another cup of coffee as they waited.

CHAPTER TWENTY-FIVE

After the last vehicle left Cold Water Creek Ranch, Hilda sat with Sharon and Chris for a cup of coffee. When she finished her's, she rinsed the cup and put it in the dishwasher. She sighed and said, "I'm tuckered out. I think I'll go rest for a while if you don't mind."

"I'm not surprised at all, Hilda. How long were you up last night baking cookies?" Sharon asked.

"I think I got the kitchen cleaned up around midnight or so," Hilda answered. "I couldn't sleep so thought I'd make myself useful."

"I'm sure everyone appreciated the cookies. But you really didn't have to do that," Sharon told her.

"Well, I do make pretty good ones and I just thought I'd give everyone a treat after all we've been through. It's going to be a long drive for them. But, if you don't mind, I think I'd like to take a little nap."

Hilda went back to the room she'd been using and laid down on the bed. She was asleep in seconds.

Todd came in from the barn and saw his parents sitting at the kitchen table staring out the large windows at the view of the meadow. "Can I talk to you guys?" he asked.

"Sure, what's up?" Chris asked.

"I just wanted to talk to you about Hilda. I heard her place is gone. She doesn't have a place to live now. She's the closest thing I have to a grandmother and I'd love it if she could stay here with us. The grandparent's rooms are not being used now since my grandparents died. She wouldn't be any trouble. And she does make the best cookies in the world. What do you think?"

Sharon looked over at Chris with one eyebrow raised. They had already decided to ask her but they wanted to see how Todd felt about it first. She smiled at her son. "Your dad and I already talked about that but wanted to make sure you'd be comfortable with it. The one to convince is Hilda. She's an independent lady, you know. She's used to living alone in her own place. We're not sure how she'll feel about it but we'll ask her when the time feels right, okay?"

"Super, Mom!" Todd smiled happily at his parents. "Guess great minds think alike. I loved her chicken casserole too. Wonder what else she can fix? Bet it's just as good. Mom, if you had someone like her to help you, you'd have a lot more time. Maybe she can help you with some of the barn paperwork too. Just a thought. Her help in the kitchen would really help you. I know you come in after working all day and have dinner to fix every night."

"I hadn't thought of that, but you're right. Maybe asking her for her help will help convince her to stay," Chris suggested. "We don't know what her children are going to tell her now that her place is gone. They may ask her to move in with one of them."

"We had a lot of time to talk while we were stuck in that canyon," Todd told them. "She already told us she doesn't want to live with either of 'em. Her son owns his own business and with his kids gone he and his wife travel a lot. She'd be there alone so much of the time. She told us she'd rather be in her own home alone than stay in someone else's home by herself. Her daughter has two kids in college and they troop in and out all the time. All the bedrooms in their house are on the second floor. Hilda told us she could make the trip upstairs only once a day. She wouldn't be able to have her little naps like she's used to if she stayed there. She couldn't even catch a nap on the couch in the living room because her daughter keeps that as a show-room only. Nobody uses it except for company."

"Well, we'll talk to her when the time is right. We're going to have to take her home sometime soon. I'm sure she wants to see what her place looks like even if it breaks her heart. Do you want to go with us when I take her over there?" Sharon asked.

"Yes," Todd said sadly. "I don't know how I would feel walking through this house all burned up. She'll probably need our support when she goes over there and I want to be there for her. She really took care of us kids in the canyon."

Chris looked at Todd with interest. "What did you guys do while you were stuck there?"

"Hilda had us all sitting in a circle lots of the time. We started out with everyone talking about their mother and father, telling what it was like at home. That was where we all wished we were at the time, you know. She just kept coming up with things like that to talk about, one after another. I really got to know everybody pretty well from that. Hilda even talked about her life with Jan and her own kids. That's how I knew she didn't want to live with them now. It kept us thinking so we didn't worry so much about being away from home and being cold or hungry. She kept us laughing too. She's really funny, you know," Todd said. "We also talked about the horses, especially after the cougar thing. It was amazing to watch ten horses chasing that big cat. He was spitting and snarling the whole way out of the canyon too."

"Sounds like you got to know her pretty well then," Sharon said.

"Mom, she was wonderful. Some of the girls were scared at night. She would hug them and talk to them until they stopped crying. Having her was great. I don't know what we kids would have done without her there."

Two hours later Hilda stepped out of the bedroom and come into the kitchen looking for Sharon. Todd had fallen asleep on the couch watching TV. She didn't want to wake him so she stepped out the mudroom door and headed for the barn. She found Sharon there in her office.

"I don't want to bother you, but I'd really like to get back to my house and see if there's anything there I can rescue," she said. "And, thank you for washing my clothes. You didn't have to do that."

"Oh," Sharon said as she looked up. "It was no bother. I was washing Todd's clothes and a load of my own so I added your things to ours. Do you think you are ready to go over there?"

"No, not really, but it's something I have to do and we might as well get it over with," Hilda admitted. "I'm afraid I won't find much, but I keep hoping…."

Sharon stepped around her desk and put her arm around Hilda's shoulder. "Let's go get Todd. He wants to go with us," she said.

Ten minutes later the three of them stood on what had been the porch of Hilda's home for the past 40 years. There wasn't much left. The rock fireplace and chimney were the tallest things left standing. They could see rubble where the barns and outbuildings had been. The metal corral panels were twisted from the heat but still where Jan put them so many years ago. Hilda looked around with tears in her eyes, trying hard not to break down.

"There's not much left of the past 40 years, is there?" Hilda said sadly. She walked carefully into her living room around burned wood and the springs from her sofa. She made her way into what had been her bedroom before she saw the burned wood she thought was her dresser. The mirror was in scorched pieces next to it. She thought she saw something under what was left of the dresser and used a piece of burned wood she found to lift it up. There was something there. She fished it out of it's hiding place and blew the ash and grime off it. It was a photograph that was taken of her and Jan on their wedding day. The glass was filthy and broken, the frame scorched but it had survived somehow while all else around it burned. Tears streamed down her cheeks as she looked at the photo.

Todd saw and came up behind her and put his arm around her shoulder. She turned and buried her face in his chest, apologizing for getting emotional. Sharon came over and took the photograph from her. "We'll get it reframed," she told her.

It took Hilda a few minutes to regain her composure. She continued to apologize for that. "From the looks of it, the only thing I have left is this photograph, Desperado, and Anabella. All the pictures of my children are gone. All the pictures of our horses are gone. All the pictures of this home and our ranch are gone. There's nothing left here. I didn't expect it to hit me so hard," she finally said when she caught her breath.

"Let's clear out of here for now," Sharon suggested. "You and I need to do some shopping. You can't wear those same clothes day in and day out. We can drop Todd off at the ranch and head for Boulder. I love shopping, don't you?" She was trying hard to get Hilda's mind off the tragic loss.

"Yes, let's do," Hilda replied, pulling herself up and straightening her shoulders. "We have a lot of shopping to do. Let's get at it. I have money in the bank and this place is insured. Some things can't be replaced, but I need to replace the things that can."

CHAPTER TWENTY-SIX

David Nyland and Jessica Lawrence were found in a park outside the city of Nassau by park security after the park closed. They were taken to the local police station. They had changed clothing but nothing could hide Mr. Nyland's appearance. The floppy brimmed hat he wore did not cover the frizzy red hair and bird beak nose of his. Nyland and Jessica couldn't come up with a good reason for sleeping in the park after closing time. The duty officer realized quickly they were wanted so he called the Police Headquarters to let them know they'd been picked up. Detectives Padilla and Arias identified him immediately.

Under questioning, Nyland cracked. He hoped to protect Jessica so he told the officers everything they wanted to know. He admitted doing the arson job in Colorado. He told the two detectives everything he knew hoping for a lighter sentence. There were lots of stops and starts in the conversation while the Detectives communicated with the District Attorney in Colorado. He named Henry Babcock as the man who hired him for the arson job. He had done jobs for Babcock in the past and gave them all the details. He also told them he was in fear for his life and that of his lady friend. He told them he was positive the bombing at the hotel was intended for him. The switch up of tables in the hotel dining room was a last minute thing. He'd heard rumors that Henry Babcock didn't tolerate failure. He felt sure the man would try again until he succeeded.

Jessica had done no wrong and committed no crime. All she wanted was to get away from this island and get back home to Colorado where she felt safe. She wanted no part of David Nyland after this. She told the detectives everything she knew, which wasn't much. They kept her in protective custody until the State Department in Washington DC gave them permission to bring her and Nyland back home to Denver.

The only thing left for Padilla and Arias was to arrest Henry Babcock. They were itching to get that done as soon as possible.

Detective Padilla had numerous conversations with the Beau Collier, the District Attorney in Colorado. There were a few complications in the Nyland case. He was wanted for Arson, Murder and the Destruction of Public Property in the United States. The State Department in Washington, DC was working with the Bahamian government on extradition so he could be returned to Colorado and face trial. The problem was there were deaths in the Bahamas as well. He was not directly, but indirectly, responsible for them and the destruction at The Reef Hotel. Both countries wanted a piece of his miserable hide.

It wasn't until the scuba diver was found washed up on the beach and his hotel room was searched that the identity of the bomber was discovered. Evidence gathered in his hotel room was pretty clear. He was the maker of the bomb. Photos of him were shown to the staff at The Reef Hotel and several kitchen workers identified him as being there the day of the bombing. One of the other waiters was sure he was the man he saw fiddling with the table that blew up that night.

Nyland was kept in solitary confinement in the jail at Police Headquarters in Nassau. He was also kept on suicide watch to ensure one of the officers checked on him every 15 minutes around the clock because of the attempt on his life. They were getting tired of him. He required far too much time. Police Chief Oxley complained bitterly to the government officials about keeping him. They finally agreed to allow the extradition.

Detectives Padillo and Arias stayed at The Reef Hotel as a guest of Mr. Vickers. He had plenty of rooms available. After the bombing, guests fled the hotel like rats leaving a sinking ship. He even lost some of the staff because of their fear from the bombing. Mr. Vickers had so much on his own plate, he stayed in one room himself so he didn't have to take the time to drive home. Engineers thoroughly checked the hotel and declared it safe. Mr. Vickers worked with the owners to get contractors in to rebuild damaged areas. He moved the fine dining into a banquet room across the hall from the room being repaired. A few guests scheduled to arrive canceled their reservations after hearing about the bomb in the dining room, but most did not. The guests who left the hotel because of the bomb were quickly replaced with new guests. Business as usual, sort of.

Chief Oxley himself called Detective Padilla when his government decided to release Nyland into their custody. He'd already been in touch with Beau Collier so Collier had tickets wired to Padilla for the two detectives plus Nyland and his girlfriend from Nassau to Denver through Miami. The flights left the next morning.

Detectives Padilla and Arias hosted Mr. Vickers and his wife for dinner that night before they packed their stuff for departure the next day. They had the property of Nyland and his girlfriend packed and ready to go along with them. No sense leaving it all in the hands of Mr. Vickers to deal with. He certainly had enough to deal with.

At Police Headquarters in Nassau the following morning, Police Chief Oxley himself escorted Nyland and Jessica out of lock-up to the front entrance to meet with Padilla and Arias. Jessica was not handcuffed and back in her civilian clothes. Nyland, on the other hand, was in jail garb and shackled. His wrists were cuffed and cuffed to a chain around his waist. Both legs were also shackled together. He walked carefully so he didn't trip himself. Two police cruisers waited at the curb behind the rental car of Padilla and Arias. The Chief shook hands with the detectives and wished them luck on their journey back to Denver. Police officers of the Bahamian government escorted Nyland and Jessica to separate vehicles and led the convoy to the airport. Nyland was assisted to the security area, passed through customs and was seated ahead of all other passengers on the flight. The flight attendant provided a lap blanket to cover his shackles so his appearance on the flight would not bother other passengers onboard. Arias sat in the window seat, Nyland in the center and Padilla sat on the aisle of the first row of seats. Once they were situated, the flight attendants boarded other passengers for the flight.

It was a short hop to Miami from Nassau. At Miami International Airport, Arias, Nyland, Padilla, and Jessica were the last passengers off the plane. Jessica sulked. Finally, Padilla spoke to her. "Listen, you are on this flight as the guest of the State of Colorado. The least you could do is stop sulking and follow orders. When we get off this plane we are going to the Airport Police Security Area at the airport to wait for the flight to Denver. Stick close to us and everything will go well. Once we get you to Denver, you are on your own. You can do whatever you want. If we need you for trial, make yourself available. If you leave town, let us know and make sure we have some way to reach you. Do you understand?"

Jessica looked down at her shoes. "I don't know how I got mixed up in all this. I'm sorry to be such a bother. Yes, I understand and will cooperate." She looked up at Officer Padilla then squinted her eyes a little. "And, please tell the State of Colorado thank you for me."

Airport Security officers met the plane to escort the group through a private customs area and then to the Airport Security offices to wait for the plane to Denver. Walking along the open corridor toward customs, they were in full view of many passengers and airport personnel. Nyland walked slowly so he didn't trip on the shackles. He coughed, dipping his head low to cover his mouth with one fist chained to his waist.

At that precise second, the window of the terminal across from the group exploded into thousands of glass shards and a bullet smacked into the concrete wall where Nyland's head had been a nanosecond earlier.

Nyland dropped flat to the floor. So did everyone in the group. Other passengers grabbed their luggage and ran screaming away from the area. Some just dropped their luggage and ran. Armed Security Policemen ran outside the terminal heading across the street to the parking structure. That's where those present felt the bullet had to come from. Policemen called for assistance on their shoulder radios and soon the entire area was swarming with officers, both from the City of Miami and Airport Police. Nyland, his detective escorts, and Jessica were rushed into a warren of passages inside the terminal building that was unknown to regular passengers. One of the Airport cops found a wheelchair and shoved Nyland into it so they could make better time getting around with him.

They were taken to an interior Customs Office. Arias pulled three passports from his breast pocket. One was his, one was Nyland's and one was Jessica's. Mr. Vickers had retrieved them for the Officers from the hotel registration area where they were stored upon check-in at the hotel. Padilla pulled the extradition orders from his breast pocket along with his own passport. The Customs Agents looked over the paperwork and signed them off to continue their journey.

The Airport Police took the group to their own security area in the terminal to wait. In the meantime, police officers swarmed throughout the public areas of the terminal and the parking structure across the street. There were several spots from which a sniper could have fired that shot. Camera footage from the security cameras in the garage was being reviewed. Police found several of the cameras had been recently damaged and produced no footage at all. Numerous cars left that garage shortly after the shot was fired but it was impossible to determine if those cars had been anywhere near the locations that could have been used. Every vehicle in the garage and every one that left after the shot was fired had to be checked out. The Miami Chief of Police, along with the Chief of the Airport Police followed the investigation closely. They were frustrated. This sniper was very careful, very skillful, and very cagey. He or she knew the business and how to cover his or her tracks.

Padilla, sitting close to the radio inside the Security Police offices in the terminal, heard report after report coming in from officers working the investigation. All he could think was if this was another of Henry Babcock's ideas, he was going to be very disappointed again. They found the last man who missed the mark washed up on the shores of the Bahamas. He was trying very hard to silence Nyland. What was going to happen to this sniper who also failed? What exactly did Nyland have on him anyway? He and Arias concurred that getting Nyland back to Denver and in protective custody as soon as possible was urgent. It occurred to both of them that Mr. Babcock was a ruthless sociopath. Would he try to blow up an airliner with them and Nyland on it just to protect himself? Both Detectives were a lot more nervous about the flight home.

CHAPTER TWENTY-SEVEN

Walter and Mike went to the gate to help Charles Carnegie through the phalanx of reporters when he arrived at the ranch with Rose and Maryann Wilcox, Becky Howard, and his wife, Celeste. Charles parked near the house and they all went inside for a discussion before facing the chaos outside.

"I'll go talk to the reporters first. Maybe I can get them to agree to an informal Press Conference format for this. I can handle those pretty well. I can introduce all of us and then take questions as they come. Some will be directed to you, youngsters. Just answer their questions as best as you can. If you need help, we'll all be there to help. Okay?" Charles said to the group.

Walter was the only one of the group to watch Charles Carnegie in action at the Press Conference in Colorado. He was all for the idea and gave the others his opinion. Everyone agreed. Charles and Walter went outside and invited the reporters and their cameramen onto the ranch. They were going to set up the conference on the back patio of the ranch house. The reporters were promised access to the horses after they interviewed the kids.

Charles and Celeste, Mike and Ginny, Walter and Caroline and Rose walked out with Brody, Maryann, and Becky. They stood back while Charles talked to the reporters and gave their names. He told them each name, then spelled it for the reporters so they could get the right spelling in their stories. He introduced the youngsters last. Once the introductions were over, reporters hands flew in the air. Charles asked one at a time for their questions.

Several of the reporters in California had heard rumors of the cougar in the canyon with ten horses, nine young people, and one elderly woman. They were excited to get that story down for their pieces on TV and in newspapers.

Brody told the story. At the time, none of the kids or Hilda were aware of the cat but the horses certainly were. The cat crept into the canyon very early in the morning. Brody told about the sudden and forceful attack all ten horses made on the cougar, led by Desperado. He told them how the large cougar ran snarling and spitting out of the canyon with ten horses on his tail. He showed the reporters with his hands the size of the cougar's footprints they found only a few feet from where they lay sleeping. He explained Desperado was owned by the elderly woman with them but was ridden in the shows by Todd O'Neal, the son of the ranch owner in Colorado where they were riding. He went on to tell the reporters how Desperado led them through the smoke to the elderly woman's home to get her, stopped in the barn to let his own mother out of her barn stall, then lead them to that isolated canyon where they found safety from the fire. Brody didn't have to embellish the story for everyone to realize what a hero Desperado was, even if he was just a horse.

Questions went on for nearly an hour. Becky, Maryann, and Brody were getting tired by that time. The questions of how they came to be there were answered. Questions about how they did at the Nationals were answered. Ginny Hartley brought out one of her own National Championship trophies to show them. The ones Becky and Maryann brought home looked exactly the same but were packed away at that moment. Questions about what they had been doing when the fire broke out were answered. The entire story of the frightening run from the wildfire was hashed and re-hashed a bit. They described how the firemen came to their rescue and got them back to safety. They gave the Fire and Forestry Service credit for what they'd done. What the kids and Hilda did while they were trapped in the canyon was described in some detail. They told how happy they were when the Fire Department dropped supplies in for them until they could come to get the group out. In the kids' eyes, the Fire Department, Forestry Department, and the horses were the heroes in this, and none more than Desperado. Had he not found them a safe place to go, they wouldn't have survived at all.

As soon as the questions were answered, the reporters and their cameramen were taken to the main show barn and allowed to see all of the horses from the canyon that were on the Hartley Ranch. Most of them especially wanted to see Prince Ali. Becky took him out of his stall and turned him out in the arena so they all had a good look at him. Ali showed a few scorch marks on his backside. Becky explained she and Ali were at the rear of the pack to keep the others moving as fast as possible and keep them bunched together. She also showed them the tee shirt she was wearing during the run from the fire. It had several small burn marks in it where embers were blown onto her clothing. Ali gained points for how beautifully he showed off for the reporters. He was always a ham. He took the opportunity to show some of his best moves. Reporters around the arena were entranced with the cougar story and could hardly believe ten horses would chase a full grown mountain lion when they should have been running away from it. That was the talk of the day.

Becky finally had a moment to speak her mind. "You know, lots of people say Arabian horses are silly, spooky, high strung horses they wouldn't own themselves and certainly not let their children ride. I'm going to tell you a few things about them. They are highly intelligent. They are smart! They also form an attachment to people like no other breed. They love people! They were raised by people who brought them right into their own living rooms with their wives and kids. The Arab people did that for generations with these horses. Their tents were their homes and the horses lived inside with them. Can you imagine bringing a horse into your living room? They learned to be careful where they stepped so they didn't step on babies or kids' toes. They learned to love the people who cared for them. The horses we had in our group had their own special people with them and they looked out for us. Desperado went for his owner with no one telling him to. He wasn't going to leave her to burn up in the fire. He got his own mother out of there so she didn't burn up in the fire either. They all followed his lead because they seemed to know he would lead them to safety and they all had their special people riding them. So, don't ever let anyone tell you Arabian horses are nervous, flighty or high strung. They are not! And these ten horses saved ten human lives besides their own."

Becky didn't realize several cameramen had her on camera when she gave that speech. That was part of the evening news broadcasts that night along with a video of Prince Ali strutting his stuff in the arena and clips of the other kids answering questions for the reporters.

Melissa, Suzie, Heidi, and Kathy came to the ranch with their parents before the reporters left. Ginny Hartley made a few quick phone calls from her barn office about the news people. Since the impromptu Press Conference Charles Carnegie put on, the reporters had been easy to deal with and really curious about the kids and their horses. Becky put Ali back in his stall and the other girls brought out their horses and turned them out in the arena. They stood along the arena rails and talked about their horses with the reporters there. The cameramen had additional shots to process for the day's news on all stations. Every horse in the group had a scorch mark or two and Heidi brought the tee-shirt she was wearing the day the fire broke out. She showed it to the reporters so they could see the small burn holes in the back and the sleeves. That made the evening news as well. The girls also told the reporters about their successes in the show ring at the Youth Nationals show in Albuquerque the week before the fire. Every one of the horses had a Champion, Reserve Champion, Third Place, and Top Ten awards for the week before the disaster. Not only were they brave but they were Champions too!

When the decision was made to talk to the reporters in California, Ginny got on the phone to Chris O'Neal in Colorado and filled him in. "You might as well talk to them instead of dodging them. They are only doing their jobs. Take it as an opportunity to tell about those brave horses and brave kids," she told him.

Chris talked to the huddle of reporters hanging around his front gate. He promised to let them in for a few minutes when he had time to talk to his wife and son and their guest, the owner of one of the horses involved. He promised to get the other local kid and his parents over if they were able to join the group.

Sharon called Mrs. Reeves and explained what they were doing. Since Charlie and Aces High were part of the group trapped in the canyon, she thought it might give Todd some help if Charlie came over with his parents and talked to the reporters.

About the same time the reporters were asking Brody, Maryann, and Becky the questions in California, another group of reporters were asking Todd and Charlie the same questions in Colorado. Todd tended not to put so much emphasis on the bravery of Desperado but Charlie did his best to make his opinion on the matter clear. Desperado was the hero of a lifetime for him.

Todd had a sinking feeling in his gut whenever he thought about it. If Desperado was worth more because of his wins, how much more would he be worth because of his bravery? It was all slipping so far out of his reach and out of his control and it made him sadder and sadder.

Hilda, another one of the group stuck in the canyon for so long, made no bones about her feelings on the matter. Desperado saved lives that day by taking them to a place of safety. He'd also saved her life when he turned toward the fire to get her before the fire overran her home, and saved his own mother as well when he should have been running away from the danger. Hilda took credit for breeding Desperado and let it be known that she and her deceased husband thought the horse was the finest horse they'd bred in over 40 years. He was her lifetime achievement wrapped up in a single horsehide and she was very proud of him.

After all the questions were answered, Desperado, Anabella, and Aces High were taken out of their stalls so the reporters could see them. Sharon also brought out Magic, the horse Brody rode that day. The four horses were no worse for the wear and were in good spirits. The cameras loved them and they were added to the broadcasts for later with the photos from California.

The upshot of the broadcasts was an upward tick in the interest in Arabian horses across the nation. Kids wanted their own Arabian horses. Parents went to local breeders for lessons and eventually purchased horses for their children. Men and women who'd always wanted a horse in their lives went to see available Arabian horses. Rescues who specialized in Arabian horses that needed new homes found good ones among those newly interested people. It was a great time for the Arabian horse in America, thanks to the bravery of ten horses, nine young people, and one elderly woman. And who knew what was next on the horizon?

CHAPTER TWENTY-EIGHT

The flight to Denver was delayed two hours. Two Air Marshals volunteered for the flight and were equipped with rubber bullets and real ones just in case. Passengers for the flight were screened very closely. Under the circumstances, they all put up with the screening which included checking for gunshot residue on their clothing, arms, hands, and faces before they were allowed to board the plane. There were a couple of sportsmen on the flight who brought guns with them for hunting. Their ultimate destinations were in Alaska, Montana, and Wyoming. Their guns were checked through, checked by airline personnel privately for recent firing, and loaded in the belly of the plane. Bomb-sniffing dogs were used to check the baggage in the baggage hold before the plane was certified for take-off.

Under the circumstances, Padilla and Arias were both very nervous about this flight but felt much better after talking to the Air Marshals who boarded the flight with them. As was done before, Arias and Padilla with Nyland were boarded before any other passengers. The Air Marshals and Nyland's girlfriend were next. When they were ready, the balance of the passengers for the flight were finally allowed to board the plane.

Despite the misgivings of Padilla and Arias and the Air Marshals, the flight to Denver was a boring five hours long. Nothing happened. The plane did not blow up from an explosive in the baggage department. No missile hit the plane and brought it down. They landed in Denver on schedule and as usual. Regular passengers were allowed to get off the plane first. The Air Marshals and Padilla with Arias deplaned with Nyland and Jessica. She never spoke one word to Nyland since they left the Police Station in Nassau.

They were met at the terminal entrance by Beau Collier and several members of the Denver P.D. Beau wanted a word with Padilla and Arias and he wanted a chance to talk to Jessica. The Denver Officers whisked Nyland off into a patrol car on his way to lock-up at the Denver P.D. headquarters where he would be put back on suicide watch with an officer checking on him every 15 minutes until he left their custody.

Beau Collier pulled Jessica aside to talk to her. "I understand this has been quite an ordeal for you. I don't blame you for being upset. I just need you to talk to me about it for a minute," he told her.

"What in the heck do you want me to say? I was stupid. I got mixed up with the wrong guy. I'm going to be sorry about this for the rest of my life," she told him, not able to meet his eyes.

"Look at me, will you?" he asked her. "Lots of women make mistakes. It's not a crime unless they are unwilling to help us put away the men who lead them into trouble. I understand you have been very cooperative. What I need from you is your address and your phone numbers so we can reach you if we need you to testify during his trial. I realize you didn't know much, but what you do know may help us. Are you at least willing to do that?" he smiled at her with his best political campaign winning smile.

She looked at him with a sheepish grin. He was charming, after all. "Of course. I will leave you with my address, one for my mother and all my phone numbers. I'd be glad to testify to what little I know just to get on with my life. Thank you for not treating me like a criminal."

With that, Jessica left the airport free as a bird. When she stepped outside into the sunlight, she looked down at her left hand and admired the large diamond sparkling on her ring finger there. She wondered how much she could get for that and some of the other jewelry David Nyland had showered her with over the past few months. She smiled as she thought of all that lovely money.

Nyland was another story altogether. He was stuffed in a police cruiser and hauled off to police headquarters and a very small jail cell until his trial came up. He was allowed his one phone call, which went to a sleazy lawyer who'd agreed to take his case. He had no access to money so he had to work with what was in his checking account at the time. The rest of his money was in accounts offshore where account numbers and passwords were needed for access. That was hidden money and he would never use the Police Department phone to call for it. The 15-minute check-ups gave him some comfort. He knew Henry Babcock without a doubt wanted him dead.

Beau Collier interviewed David Nyland the following day. He needed concrete proof that Henry Babcock was behind all the terror and the destruction. Nyland gave him as much information on Babcock as he had willingly. He gave up bank account numbers and told him about various deposits made by wire transfer for jobs he'd done for Mr. Babcock. He picked Babcock's photo out of a six-photo lineup of businessmen in suits. He'd only met the man one time, but he never forgot that face or those cold eyes. He knew if he gave law enforcement enough information they could verify, it might get Mr. Babcock put somewhere he couldn't reach him. But he didn't want to give up all his accounts. He'd done work for others besides Babcock. If there was a chance of him getting out of jail before he died, he wanted that money to live on. He would use his local accounts to pay his local lawyer, then get him to grab money out of one off-shore account so he could buy a real defense. That account had no previous wire transfers from any of his clients so if law enforcement found out about it, they couldn't find the sources and his clients would be protected. He used many names and numbers to keep track and they were stored all in his head. He didn't write things down so no one could find them. He was very careful about some things but he'd really done a bad job on the tree fire.

The District Attorney began sifting through the paperwork found in Nyland's townhouse. They found Nyland's fire making materials and evidence of his lavish lifestyle but nothing to show where the money originated except for a confirmation of the wire transfer Babcock made in addition to the package of cash he'd sent Nyland for burning his trees. They found the map Babcock sent him showing him the location of the four trees he wanted burned down. That would need confirmation it was drawn by Babcock himself, but they needed to get him into custody to have a handwriting expert go over it. With the information he'd gotten from his interview with Nyland, the identification of Babcock that Nyland gave him, and the wire transfer confirmation, he talked to the State Attorney General and got an arrest warrant for Mr. Henry Babcock of San Francisco, California. He called Detective Padilla. "You and Arias up for another flight?" he asked when Padilla answered his phone.

"As long as it's not to the Bahamas without my wife," quipped Padilla. "I'm getting no end of grief about that."

"Let's wrap this arson case up. We have enough information about the Arsonist and who hired him to get this into court and get convictions for both of them. I need you and Arias to take an arrest warrant to San Francisco and pick up Henry Babcock," Beau Collier told him. "Our Attorney General has already been in touch with his counterpart in California. It's a go."

"Wow, that was fast," Padilla said. "Let's get us some more convictions!"

Padilla and Arias were on a flight from Denver to San Francisco two hours later. It was a short flight of an hour and a half. They were met at the terminal by two San Francisco Police Detectives who drove them to Babcock's headquarters building. They passed by the reception desk and all four of them took the elevator to the top floor. They brushed right on by Mr. Babcock's protesting secretary and stormed into his private office. Henry Babcock was on the phone when they entered. Padilla walked to his desk and pushed the receiver switch on the phone to disconnect the call. "Mr. Henry Babcock, I presume?" he said to the man seated at the desk.

Henry was furious at the interruption. His face got very red very quickly. "How dare you barge into my office!" he screamed at the four men.

All four of the men turned the lapels of their jackets around so Mr. Babcock could see their badges. They said nothing. The blood drained from Henry's face as quickly as it rose up. "What do you want?" he asked.

Padilla told him, "Stand up, Mr. Babcock, and turn around. I need to handcuff you. You are under arrest for arson, murder, and destruction of public property. I will leave a copy of the warrant on your desk here," as he laid the warrant in front of the man.

"You can't do this to me!" Henry tried to scream at them but it came out like a squawk.

"Yes, we can. And these fine officers of the San Francisco Police Department are here to see we do it right. Please stand up and turn around. Detective Arias will read you your rights. We have a plane to catch so let's get on with this," Padilla said sternly.

Henry Babcock looked like he was about to faint, but slowly pushed himself back from his desk and stood up. He turned around and looked out the window behind his desk at the rest of the City by the Bay he loved so much. While he soaked in the view for perhaps the last time, Padilla came up behind him and snapped on the handcuffs, then spun him around. He held one of Babcock's arms while Arias held the other and the four men escorted him out of his office, down the elevator, and into the squad car at the curb. The San Francisco cops drove them back to the airport and escorted them to their flight, not leaving until Henry Babcock was seated on the plane.

Padilla leaned over Babcock to talk to Arias. "I checked with the Credit Union when we got back from the Bahamas. I've got enough to take my wife on that vacation. I called Mr. Vickers at The Reef. He said he would take care of us, just name the dates. I can't wait to call him after we're done here. Have you thought about joining us for a week of laying around with your wife?"

"Heck, yes. Pauline and I will join you if I have to borrow the money," Arias said. Let's have dinner together and go over some dates. I'm looking forward to it after this case."

CHAPTER TWENTY-NINE

With the fire controlled and nearly out, the kids back where they belonged, and the reporters not hanging around the front gate, things slowly got back to normal at Cold Water Creek Ranch. Chris got back into his training routine, Sharon got back to her paperwork, and Todd helped his dad on the ranch. Ranch employees returned to work. The only thing different now was Hilda. She agreed to stay with the O'Neal's temporarily while she thought about whether to rebuild her home on her own property. She knew it would never be the same as the one Jan built for them so many years ago. There was too much of Jan's personal hand in the construction of their home.

Her son and her daughter insisted she come live with them. Hilda rejected their pleas outright. She was not going to move in with her son and spend most of her time alone in his house. She couldn't imagine climbing the stairs more than once a day in her daughter's home and was afraid the day would come when she couldn't even make the trip once a day. Her old hips and knees were wearing out from a lifetime of use.

She enjoyed the peace and quiet of the space she occupied in the O'Neal's home. She discovered the private entrance also included a small patio where she could sit outside on a nice day and enjoy the fresh air. She came to love having her morning coffee there. It gave her a sense of privacy while at the same time allowed Chris and Sharon their own time together.

Sharon came in to make lunch for the family and found Hilda had it nearly ready. She thanked Hilda for stepping in. Hilda suggested she make that a part of her repayment to the O'Neal's for letting her stay with them temporarily. Sharon took that opportunity to extend the invitation to stay permanently. She asked if Hilda could help her in the kitchen with meals and maybe help her with some of the paperwork in the barn. Hilda couldn't believe her good fortune. She loved the O'Neal's and loved her suite of rooms in their home. She was much happier here than she'd been in her own home after Jan passed away. She didn't feel so all alone.

With Show Season still underway until late fall, Hilda needed to get copies of Desperado's registration papers. The ones she had burned in the fire. Those papers were needed with the entry forms and fees every time Desperado was entered in a show. She asked Sharon to take her into Boulder to the Arabian Horse Registry, so she could get duplicate copies. She needed to get the duplicate for Annabella too.

Sharon and Hilda planned to make it an entire day with shopping in Denver when they got Hilda's business taken care of. There were stores in Denver they both loved, but with the two-hour drive to get there, they didn't get many opportunities. It only took Hilda a few minutes to get the duplicate papers she needed, and they were off to shop. Sharon and Hilda left things in the refrigerator for Todd and Chris so they didn't starve in their absence. They had a great time in Denver, stopping in a nice restaurant for dinner before the drive home.

"You know," Hilda began, "I've really enjoyed living with you, Chris and Todd. It gives me something to do every day and its stuff I love doing. I just want you to know how much I appreciate you letting me stay with you."

Sharon smiled across the dining table at her. "We've really enjoyed having you with us too. Todd thinks of you as the grandmother he didn't get to grow up with. You spoil him with cookies! Of course, Chris and I enjoy them too. I don't remember how I ever got along without your help. You always know what needs doing and do it. I've actually had some time to read a couple of books I've wanted to read but never had time for. You're a keeper. We want you to stay."

"I do have my own income and I'd like to contribute to the household expense from now on. I use things in the house. My rooms cost you money to heat and cool. I use water and things like that so I'm going to give you a check every month when my pension money comes in. You can do what you want with it. If you don't need it for household expenses, why don't you put it away for Todd's college fund?"

"Hilda, just you being there and doing what you do is contribution enough for me. I'll talk to Chris about it, but the college fund is a good idea. I don't feel right taking money from you."

"Sharon, Jan did not leave me penniless. The insurance company is going to settle on my property and I will have that too. I think my own kids are waiting to get their hands on it but I've decided they will have to wait a while longer. I might enjoy spending it myself and I'm not going anywhere soon," she laughed.

"Chris and I will talk about it later tonight and I'll talk to you again in the morning," Sharon said. "Now let's finish up this delicious dinner while it's still hot and then get on the road for home."

Desperado spent a lot of time talking to Aces after they got home from the canyon. Aces had a "hero worship" relationship with Desperado that Desperado didn't understand. The first night home, Chris had Aces stabled directly across the aisle from Desperado. Aces spent so much time just staring at him he finally spoke up about it. *"What are you looking at, Aces?"*

"I'm so happy you were with us during the fire and all. I don't know if we'd have figured out where to go or how to survive. Thank you for leading us," Aces said quietly and almost reverently.

"Oh, for Pete's sake Aces, didn't I tell you guys I wouldn't have known where to go either if the little doe hadn't told me about the canyon? Hey, my own skin was on the line too not to mention Todd and Charlie and all the others. You took your life in your hands when we chased that cougar out of the canyon. I saw you. You were right behind me with Ali," Desperado told him.

"Yes, but it was your idea to chase him in the first place," Aces reminded him. *"I would have run the other way if you hadn't come up with that idea."*

"You give me way too much credit, Aces. I just figured if one or two of us turned the tables on him, he'd be the one running away instead of us. And, it did work didn't it?"

"Yeah, but you stepped up without anyone asking you and took the first lead out on the road so we could get home," Aces said.

"Well, I wanted to get home and we couldn't all lead. I just stepped up so we could get started. And you took over the lead when Max got tired. You took your turn at leading us through the potholes, boulders, and stumps. You did just as good a job at that as I did, or any of the rest of us," Desperado told him. *"Don't discredit yourself. You were brave and strong when you needed to be."*

"I'm not sure I ever want to go on a trail ride again after this," Aces told him.

"Oh, now. Don't be silly! You love trail rides with Charlie. You know you do! None of this would have happened if it weren't for those two silly girls. They are in California now. You stuck with me and Todd, Becky and Ali, Maryann and Quesa and the others. Todd and Brody were right. They couldn't go back to the ranch and leave those girls out in the forest like that. What would have happened to them if a bull elk stepped out in front of them? They wouldn't have known what to do. Charlie is a sensible boy. He doesn't take chances like that and you know it. Neither does Todd or Becky when she's here. We'll still have nice rides together as long as I'm here," Desperado told him.

"What do you mean, as long as you are here?" Aces asked in surprise.

"Hilda is my owner, you know. Todd is just my rider even though I love him dearly. He doesn't own me. If something happens to Hilda, her children will sell me in a flash. I won't have any choice in that nor will I have any choice where I end up. I will probably never see you or Todd again," Desperado explained with pain in his heart.

"What makes you think something is going to happen to Hilda anyway?" Aces asked.

"She's getting old. When people get as old as she is, they begin to get sick and then they die. Do you know what that means?" Desperado asked.

"Don't think I've ever thought about that. What does that mean?"

"When people die, like when other animals die, the life force goes out of them. Their spirit leaves their body and they are no more. They can't talk. They can't walk. They can't get up and they can't move. I understand people do to those dead bodies the same thing they do when their dog or cat dies. I know you've seen it. They dig a hole and put the body in it and cover it with dirt. They call it bury. The point is, they are not here with us any longer. *They can't say what is going to happen to things they own and things they loved when they lived. I think their relatives do all that. And I've heard Hilda's children talking about selling me when Hilda dies."*

"Well, Hilda is a tough lady. I don't think she is going to die anytime soon. Stop worrying about it, Desperado. Think about all the fun you will have with your Todd instead," Aces yawned. *"Think I'm going to get some sleep now. You get some yourself, okay? I don't think you are going anywhere for a long time unless it's to the next show."*

Hilda checked her calendar every morning, not just to see what day it was but she penciled in special days, like birthdays and anniversaries on her calendar. She looked and saw that Todd's birthday was in three days. That gave her time to plan. It was her habit to make the birthday person their favorite meal for dinner, bake a beautiful birthday cake and add in some ice cream and birthday candles for the celebration. Presents came after the cake and ice cream. She mentioned it to Sharon that morning after Todd left to go to the barn.

"I think his favorite dish is my chicken casserole, isn't it?" she asked Sharon. "If so, I need to go to the store for a few things, but I also need some supplies for the cake and ice cream. What are his favorite cake and ice cream?"

Sharon thought about it a minute, "You're right about the chicken casserole. We all love it. If I were to pick his favorite cake, I think it would have to be carrot cake. He does like to share his cake with Desperado you know," she laughed. "Probably with the cream cheese icing and vanilla bean ice cream. That just sounds wonderful. How about we go this morning. I'll catch up on my paperwork this afternoon."

Hilda spent a lot of time thinking about her circumstances early in the morning while she had her coffee on her private patio. She was almost 80 years old and she had no idea how much time she had left. Her bank account was more than enough to meet her personal needs. She'd talked to the insurance company about the destruction of her property and knew that would add another sizeable amount to it. Sadly, she also understood that her own children had no interest in the property they'd been raised on or the horses she owned. They'd both moved away and set up their own lives and didn't have much time for her or the things they'd been raised with. It had always been Jan's dream that his son would take over the breeding and training business he started all those years ago.

Her son was not interested. He started his own successful business and spent all his energies on that with no time left for horses, breeding, training or much else. His wife wasn't raised with horses and had no interest in them. She loved to travel. After their children left home she spent her time traveling with her husband as he worked on his business. In between business trips, they visited far off places around the world.

Her daughter left for college in Denver right after high school. She met and married her husband before she graduated. She dropped out of college to begin her family and regretted never finishing. Because of that, she insisted her own children get their education. She and her husband moved so they were close to the University. Her kids could live at home while getting their education. She and her husband poured all their extra money into that. Their money went for tuition, books, and lab fees at the University and the cars they bought for the kids to get them there. Fortunately, her husband was a high-level executive with a computer firm and made plenty of money.

Neither of her children needed money. They were both doing very well. If she left everything to them, they would sell it immediately. The land, the horses and everything she and Jan had lived for would be gone. It made her sad. Nothing she and Jan worked for so hard and for so many years would continue. Their legacy would be parceled out and sold in an instant.

It occurred to her that there might be a way to preserve that legacy. She could leave them each some money but the land and the horses she could leave to someone who would appreciate them more.

Desperado, the best horse they'd ever bred, should go to someone who would appreciate him for what he is. Todd loves that horse. He will take care of him and do the right things with him. He would not be sold and taken away so Todd could never see him again.

Annabella was the result of many years of breeding. She and Jan studied pedigrees, did inciteful breeding for several generations to produce her. She was still young enough to have a few more foals.

Her 40 acres was right down the road from Cold Water Creek Ranch. It might make a wonderful home for Todd in a few years and might help Chris and Sharon in the meantime. They would never cut it up and sell off the pieces. They appreciated the value of the land in a way her children did not.

She made her decision. She didn't need to put the ownership of the horses in her will. She had their registration papers in her hand. All she had to do was sign off the back and hand them over to whoever she chose. She would have to visit the lawyer to provide for the money for her children and leave the land to those she wanted to have it.

CHAPTER THIRTY

When Todd woke up three days later he was excited. It was his fifteenth birthday and his dad promised to go for a trail ride with him. They didn't get to do that very often and Todd really enjoyed spending time away from the ranch with his Dad.

He came downstairs dressed and ready to go and had a quick breakfast of cold cereal at the kitchen table while his parents finished their coffee.

"Dad, where do you want to ride today?" he asked eagerly.

"There are several places that might be fun," his dad said. "We could cross the highway and ride south toward the Flatirons if you want. I don't think you and I ever rode that direction."

"Oh, man, that would be fun! How long do you think it would take us to get to the Flatirons?" Todd asked him.

"I don't know if we can get all the way to the Flatirons in one day, Todd. They are about twenty miles from here. That would make a forty mile ride in one day. We're not riding endurance horses, you know," he said with a laugh. "You're going to have to take your phone with us. We might need the GPS to get us back home."

"Aren't there trails in that area you used to ride with Mom?" Todd asked.

"Sure there are, but it's been a few years since we rode that way, you know. I don't think your Mom and I had much of a chance to get away on horseback for very long since you were born. That's been fifteen years now, son!" Chris reminded him.

Todd grinned at his dad. "I know. Guess I'm growing up," he laughed. "Let's get going. Gramma Hilda sort of let me know there might be a nice dinner tonight when we get back. I can't wait to see what she's planned for my birthday. I don't know how we got along without her for so long. She's been a big help to Mom and she sure knows her way around a kitchen."

"You're right Todd. She's been a big help here. I'm glad we asked her to stay with us," Sharon said. "Now you two get going. She and I've got work to do."

Todd and Chris walked to the barn and began brushing down their horses before tacking them up for the ride. The minute they walked out the mudroom door, Hilda walked into the kitchen. She pulled the cream cheese out of the refrigerator to soften, started peeling and grating the carrots and soaking the raisins. Her carrot cake was famous. It was spicy and moist and her cream cheese frosting about the best anyone ever tasted.

Chris and Todd walked down the highway a short way until Chris saw the trail on the opposite side. They waited for an opening in the traffic and crossed to the east side of the highway. The trail they followed meandered into the woods and around settlements most of the way. They rode side by side and talked. They didn't get a lot of time for talking like this. Todd told his dad he wanted to eventually take over the reins of Cold Water Creek Ranch the same way Chris had when his dad got too old to do the work. Todd wanted to go to the University of Colorado for a degree in agriculture with a minor in equine after high school. He felt it would prepare him for running the ranch better. He hoped to go to the campus in Boulder so he didn't have to leave home for school. In the meantime, he only had three more years he could ride in the Youth Division classes and he wanted to take full advantage of that. He told his dad he wanted to start working with him more closely with the training of young horses so he could learn more from him.

Chris encouraged his son's aspirations. He'd gone to California for school rather than stay at home and he saw the advantages of studying from home. He explained, however, he'd met Sharon while going to college and he never regretted that. Had he remained in Colorado for school he might never have met her at all. "She could have been swept off her feet by some California surfer type if I hadn't decided to go to school in California, you know," Chris laughed. "You just never know what's around the next corner. All you can do is be prepared for anything."

"Oh, Dad, I can't see Mom as a surfer girl," Todd laughed.

"You didn't see the woman I met then," Chris told him. "She wore her hair long and straight and wore short flowery dresses and Birkenstocks every day. She was sweet and I thought she was beautiful."

"Do you have any pictures of that?" Todd laughed. "I'd love to see those!"

"Probably somewhere we do. I'll have to find them for you sometime. When we got here to Colorado was the first time I ever saw her in jeans and boots. She was even more beautiful to me. Then I found out she could ride the hair off any of my horses and I just couldn't let her go."

The two turned back toward the ranch about noon and took their time. They talked about Desperado and how impressed Todd was with his bravery. They talked about what the kids did while they were in the canyon. They talked about anything and everything. It was one of the few times they had like that in their busy worlds and both enjoyed it and didn't want it to end. Chris was very proud of the young man his son was becoming. Todd respected his father even more after hearing about his own youth on the ranch and how he'd gradually taken over for his father as Grandpa O'Neal became older and able to do less. It was fun hearing about Grandma O'Neal too. She was gone before Todd was born so he'd never met her. Chris described how tough his mother had been and how hard she'd worked to keep the ranch going. These were stories he'd never heard before.

Desperado enjoyed the ride with Chris and Todd. The talk they had was easy and comfortable between them. Then Desperado thought he saw something that made his heart beat a little faster. Off in the distance, he saw a couple of does watching them from a small clearing. One of the does had a white marking on her face. It had to be Blaze! She survived! He was almost giddy with happiness. His steps became a little stronger and he breathed a lot easier. He hoped he would get a chance to talk to her again sometime. He felt a whole lot better knowing she'd gotten away from the fire.

When Chris and Todd got back to the ranch after their long ride, they untacked their horses, brushed them down and bathed them before putting them in their stalls. They gave their horses treats before heading for the house.

Walking through the mudroom door, the smells from the kitchen made them both hungry. They quickly stripped off their boots and walked into the kitchen. The smells there were even better and their stomachs growled. "We're really hungry, Gramma Hilda!" Todd exclaimed. "Boy, it sure smells good in here."

"Wash up," Hilda told them. "I'm about to put dinner on the table."

Chris and Todd washed their hands and faces in the kitchen sink, drying off with paper towels and hurried to sit down at the kitchen table. Sharon brought glasses of milk and sat down herself. Hilda brought out the large casserole dish in oven-gloved hands and sat with them. "Dig in!" she encouraged.

Hilda's chicken noodle casserole was even better when flavored with a good case of hunger. It was half devoured on the first round and Chris and Todd helped themselves to a second plateful. There was little talking at the table at first. Everyone was too busy eating to talk.

"Did you two have a good ride," Sharon finally asked them.

"Mom, it was the best! Dad and I don't get a chance to do that very often. I think we need to make time and maybe you should come too," Todd answered after swallowing another bite. "I've never been south-east of the ranch. The country there drops down a lot but the views are sure pretty. We didn't get to the Flatirons. I'd like to trailer the horses down and ride around them sometime. Lots of guys go there to climb the rocks. I'd just like to ride there."

"I have cake and ice cream for dessert tonight," Hilda told them. "Finish up your plates and I'll bring out the cake."

Sharon and Hilda gathered the plates from dinner and took them to the sink. Hilda pulled the cake from the refrigerator and stopped long enough to put fifteen candles on it, each candle in the middle of a tiny orange and green carrot she'd piped on the cake around the "Happy Birthday Todd." She lit the candles before bringing the cake to the table. She set the cake down in front of Todd. "Blow 'em out so we can see how many years it will take to get your wish," she encouraged him.

"You know it is one year for every time you have to blow to get them all out."

Todd smiled and blew all fifteen candles out in one breath. "Guess my wish will come true now. I don't have to wait another year or two."

Hilda handed Chris a large envelope and then she handed a similar one to Todd. "This is my gift to you. After you open it, I'll explain," she said.

Both of them slid their fingers under the envelope flap and pulled out the paper inside. Chris looked puzzled. Todd looked shocked. Sharon watched curiously. Hilda sat and smiled at them.

"Todd, this is the signed registration paperwork for Desperado. I want you to have him as your own. You've earned it. He's the best horse Jan and I ever bred and I know that Jan would agree with this. Take care of him, son. He's a treasure!"

Tears formed in Todd's eyes but he refused to let them drop. He jumped up from his chair and pulled Hilda from hers. He hugged her nearly enough to crush her but couldn't find his voice. He struggled to keep his tears and wiped a few of them off on her shoulder. He finally pulled back and held her shoulders in his hands. "Is this for real Gramma Hilda?"

"Yes, it's for real. Now git out there and hug your horse!" she told him.

Todd ran for the mudroom, pulled on his boots and ran to the barn.

Hilda looked over at Chris and Sharon. "I have some things for you too," she said. "Now let me explain. Annabella is the best mare Jan and I bred and it took us thirty-some years to get her. I don't want all that work and effort sold to just anyone with a few dollars when my time comes. I want you to have her. Jan and I studied breeding and I can help you there. We can use Annabella to produce another Desperado for you if you'll take my breeding advice. The other piece of paper in your envelope is the title to my forty acres. I don't want that parceled out. That's equally important to me. I think you and Sharon can use it to develop your breeding facility, and maybe do more boarding if you'd like. I will also help you with some of the replacement costs for barns. My hope is the facility will provide a home for Todd and his family someday. It should become part of Cold Water Creek Ranch. I've thought a lot about this so don't try to change my mind. I'm an old woman and I don't want all the years of work Jan and I put into the breeding of Arabian horses going to waste. I think you and your son are the perfect ones to pick it up and run with it after I'm gone."

Todd pulled the door open on Desperado's stall, stepped in and threw his arms around Desperado's neck. "You are mine! All mine! You aren't going anywhere! You and I can be together forever!" He pressed his face into the silken neck as he spoke. Dark stains from his tears marked Desperado's neck. Desperado was shaken. Did he hear that right? Did Todd just tell him he now belonged to Todd and he would never be shipped away from here or be sold to that horrid bunny-kicker man? When he felt Todd's tears on his neck and he felt the boy's emotion in his hug, he knew. He and Todd would always be together. He raised his head, stretched his neck and let the whole ranch know about his happiness in that scream of joy. The three adults still sitting at the kitchen table heard it and smiled at one another. Desperado turned his neck and pressed Todd's body close to his.

www.ingramcontent.com/pod-product-compliance
Lightning Source LLC
Chambersburg PA
CBHW070512260626
47161CB00004B/1531